I0698862

SAVAGE

Sherry Derr-Wille

Savage
Copyright © 2025 by Sherry Derr-Wille

All rights reserved. No part of this publication may be reproduced, distributed, or transmitted in any form or by any means, including photocopying, recording, or other electronic or mechanical methods, without the prior written permission of the author, except in the case of brief quotations embodied in critical reviews and certain other non-commercial uses permitted by copyright law.

ISBN
978-1-969642-51-7 (Paperback)
978-1-969642-50-0 (eBook)
978-1-969642-52-4 (Hardcover)

Contents

Prologue

Hunting Hawk paced his lodge. With the sunrise, he would be leaving with the young hunters and their fathers for the first hunt of the year. It was a test for the young men. Some would become accomplished hunters; others were better suited for other positions in the village. Among these young braves, were future healers, flint nappers, and leaders. It was up to him, as the leader of the hunters to define the destination of these eager young men.

Across the lodge, his life partner, Singing Bird, slept peacefully. It was late in her pregnancy, and he feared missing the most important day of his life. Soon his first born would come into the world. Be it brave or maiden, he knew he would love the child they conceived will all his heart. He'd loved Singing Bird ever since they'd been children. Their union was only natural.

"Come back to bed, my love," Singing Bird coaxed. "It will soon be dawn, the time you will be leaving for the hunt. I need you to hold me before it is time for the sun to rise on this long-expected morning.

"What if the baby is born before I return? I don't want to miss the birth of our first child."

"There is nothing to worry about. The midwife assures me the baby won't be born for at least several days. You will be home, and we will celebrate the success of the hunt, long before our child comes into the world."

Chapter One

Caleb MacAfee made his way home. He'd been in the two towns over replenishing his supplies. It would soon be planting time and long trips like this one would have to wait until the farm work was done.

Having grown up in Scotland, he never had to worry about the long trips to obtain supplies. The village near his family's keep housed many shopkeepers who gladly delivered whatever supplies were needed.

With his older brothers taking over the horse stables in Scotland, Caleb immigrated to America, to become one of the top horse breeders in the new world.

The trip to get supplies took more than a day each way. Not wanting to leave his wife and children alone for two full days, he'd left before the sun was up yesterday morning, filled his wagon, and turned back toward home before sunset.

Morning birds began singing, to coax the sun to rise above the eastern horizon. As though the birds and night animals sensed something was amiss, they became eerily silent. It didn't take long for the reason for their sudden silence.

Screams permeated the silence, and the scent of smoke filled his nostrils. He urged the team forward. As he crested the hill, he saw the smoke came from the Indian village close to his farm.

When he first arrived in the New World, they became good friends. He'd even employed some of the young men when it was time to break the horses. Men women and children were among the dead and dying littering the common area of the village.

A scream, different from the others, cut through the scene before him. This was a primal scream, the sound of a woman giving birth. Searching through the bodies, he saw Singing Bird lying in the dirt of the well-worn pathway. She was sweating profusely, and he knew she was ready to deliver, He no more than knelt beside her, when with her last breath, she pushed the baby from her body.

He quickly lifted the screaming little boy and cut the cord connecting the child with his mother, with his hunting knife. He also cut some of the material his wife ordered from the general store and used it to wrap the child against the chill of the early morning.

Torn between the child and the dead villagers, he decided to see for the safety of the child. He could come back to bury the dead. For now, his wife, Maude, would know what to do.

On the hurried trip back to the farm he thought about Maude. They met on one of his father's ships headed for the New World. She was a widow with a five-year-old son, James. Caleb knew he fell in love with both at first sight. It wasn't long before he convinced the captain of the ship to marry them. Within a year, their daughter, Elizabeth, was born. Like his family his horse farm prospered, and he was now a wealthy man.

He stopped the team in front of the house and one of his employees came to care for the horses as he took the screaming infant into the house.

It didn't take long for him to relate the story of the massacre to Maude. She gently took the child from his arms and assessed the body of the bronze-skinned baby.

"He's perfect," Maude declared. "He does need a wet nurse. I can fix a sugar tit for him, but that won't be enough. You need to go into the settlement and see if there is a nursing mother for him."

Caleb agreed and went to the stable to mount his stallion. It didn't take long for him to reach the settlement, if you could call the conglomeration of buildings a settlement. It boasted a blacksmith shop, a tavern, and an abandoned store.

Caleb's first stop was the tavern. He scanned the assortment of bar's patrons before he made his presence known.

"What you doin' in town, MacAfee? Never seen you step foot in this tavern before. You act like you're too good to drink with the likes of us."

"I'm not here to drink the swill you call whiskey. I'm looking for a nursing mother. I need a wet nurse."

"What's wrong with your wife? Did her tits dry up on you?"

As much as Caleb wanted to strike out at the man who was taunting him, he related the story of the massacre at the Indian village, and the baby who needed milk to survive.

"My wife just had a baby, but I wouldn't want no savage suckin' on her tit. Why don't you go over to the blacksmith shop. I heard Shames bought a bed slave to breed bucks, and she had a girl. I think he would be more than willing to let her go, for a price."

As much as Caleb disliked any form of slavery, he turned on his heel and headed across the dusty street to the blacksmith's shop. The place smelled of stale smoke and body sweat. It was evident the man hadn't bathed in several weeks if not months.

"Thought you had your own blacksmith, MacAfee," Shames greeted him. "Whatcha doing here?"

"I'm not here for your services. At the tavern they said you have a bed slave who is nursing. I'm here for her."

"Why would you want a bitch who can't have boys? I'm taking her and the brat to the slave market next month."

"Why I want her is none of your business. I'll give you twice what you paid for her. That's better than you'll get at the market."

Greed gleaned in Shames' eyes. "You have a deal. With that much I can get a better slave."

"What do you call her?" Caleb asked.

"I call her Bitch and the kid I call Brat."

Caleb was horrified. Rather than vent his anger, he watched as Shames took a ring of keys from a hook on the wall and unlocked a room at the back of the shop. As soon as the door opened, he saw a frightened black girl, clutching her baby tightly. She was shackled to the wall by heavy chains, and her dress was worn and tattered.

"I put my X on the papers. You belong to Master MacAfee now."

Once freed from her shackles, she got unsteadily to her feet. Protectively, held onto her child. "I just bought both of you," Caleb said, hoping she understood him. "I'll explain everything on the way back to my farm. You and the child can ride sitting in front of me."

They left Shames counting his money and gloating over having bested Caleb.

"Do you want me to rub you, don there?" the girl asked.

"No. I don't want you for that."

He explained the events of the morning and the little boy who needed her life-giving milk.

"As soon as I can ride to the county seat and sign the papers to free you and your daughter you will become part of our family. You, like the baby, will be raised in my household as my daughters. I have a son who is older than you and a daughter about your age."

"You have a wife. What will she say about this?"

"She will welcome both of you with open arms. She is a very loving and accepting woman. There is always room in our home and hearts for more children."

~ * ~

Maude MacAfee soothed the little boy as best she could. He needed to be fed, and she was unable to do so herself. She had James go out to the barn to get some milk from the cow. While he was gone, she tried to figure out how to form a nipple for the boy to suckle.

As she waited for her son to return, she thought about Caleb. She loved the big Scotsman as soon as she saw him. With no father to guide him, James loved the attention of the kindhearted man.

Their wedding on the ship was absolute perfect and as soon as they docked Caleb insisted on giving James his last name and raising him as his son.

She had no doubt Caleb would be insistent in doing the same for this little boy as well. They wanted a large family, but after the difficult birth of their daughter, those hopes were dashed.

The front door opening dissolved the memories she'd become engrossed in. With Caleb was a black girl who didn't look old enough to have a child, even though she held a small mixed-race child in her arms.

"I bought the girl and her child from Shames. Neither of them has a name so I leave that up to you. The girl is nursing, and I know the baby needs to be fed. When he is finished, we must give her attention, as I am certain Shames was a very cruel master. When we are alone, we will have to talk about the future."

Maude watched as the child/woman took the baby and pressed his lips to her breast. Without hesitation, the baby sucked naturally and drank his fill of her life-giving milk. When he finished with his feeding the little black baby began to cry. She too suckled until she was satisfied and fell asleep.

With both children sleeping soundly, Maude assessed the condition of the young girl who her husband brought into their home.

"My husband said you and your child have no proper names."

The girl looked into Maude's eyes for the first time. "Master Shamas calls me Bitch and my baby Brat."

Maude was surprised by the girl's knowledge of the English language. "Who taught you to speak English?"

"Mistress Susan. She was Master Shamas' wife, and he told her to teach me your language. That was before she got sick. I haven't seen her since before my baby was born."

"You must have been a good student; you speak very well."

"I learned much of your language before I was taken from my home. A man who said he was a missionary came and taught English to the children. He was the man who took us away and sold us into slavery."

"How horrible, but I am pleased to have another daughter, and a smart one at that. What do you know about being a Christian?"

"The missionary did speak of Jesus and the Bible, then he betrayed us. Mistress Susan read me Bible stories until she got sick. She also made certain I was clean and fed. When I didn't see her anymore, Master Shamas wouldn't allow me to bathe but he did feed me whatever leftovers he had from his meals."

Maude's heart was breaking. "I have water heating on the stove for a bath for you and my daughter, Elizabeth, is going through her old clothes to give to you. In the meantime, I will be preparing a proper meal for you."

Without hesitation or embarrassment, the girl took off her dirty rags and stepped into the luxury of the hot bath. As she did, Maude noticed the healing and more recent welts from the beatings she'd endured at Shames' hand.

"Did you hear?" she asked Caleb as she allowed the girl some privacy.

"I did. I wonder what happened to Susan. So, help me God, if Shamas killed that woman, I will make certain he pays for his crime."

"We have more to do here than to worry about Shamas. The man thinks he's able to get away with the atrocities he has inflicted. He won't be going anywhere. For now, this girl needs our name and protection. She also needs love and care. He beat her relentlessly and she has the scars to show for it. She also needs a good meal. Not only that, but we have three children to name and love."

~ * ~

Caleb watched as Maude went into the kitchen to begin preparing a nourishing meal. Elizabeth was going through her old clothing to give to the back girl when she finished her bath.

"Where is your brother?" Caleb asked his daughter.

"James brought in the cradle for the baby. They are both small enough they can share it for the time being. When he finished that, he went with some of the stable boys and grooms to bury the dead in the Indian village. How can people be so cruel? I can't believe they are all dead. I remember when Little Bird would come to the farm with her father. She was my friend and playmate."

The tears streaming down Elizabeth's face tore at Caleb's heartstrings. *When did my daughter become such a caring young woman? When did my son become a responsible young adult?*

"Can the girl and her baby stay with us? I would love to have two new sisters."

"Of course, they can stay. Although I paid for them, I plan to give them their freedom as soon as I can get to the county seat. For now, we need to talk to the girl about what name she would prefer. We can't continue calling her Bitch. It's not proper."

As they were talking, the girl came into the room, wrapped in a towel. "Can I have a real name?"

"Of course you can. Is there anything you prefer?"

"I would like to call my daughter, Susan. She was so good to me, I would like to honor her."

Caleb nodded. "That is a proper name. What would you like to be called?"

"I don't know any other names. The ones from the Bible stories do not seem proper."

"My mother told me her mother's name was Ella," Elizabeth suggested. "Since I am named for my father's mother, it would be an honor for you to be named for our mother's mother."

The girl's brown eyes reflected her pleasure at such honor.

"What about the little boy?" Ella asked.

"I've been pondering on that. Since he is going to be your new brother, I think it is only fitting that we call him Matthew Hawk.

Matthew to honor my father and Hawk to honor his father."

"How do you know the name of Matthew's father?" Elizabeth inquired.

"I recognized his mother as Singing Bird. She and Hunting Hawk were joined as life partners last year and were awaiting the birth of their son. He carries both of their genes in his body. It is only proper he should carry Hawk's name. As soon as the minister comes through town, we will have all three of them baptized."

"Our family is growing, just as we hoped it would," Maude said, as she came from the kitchen. "We built this house with the expectation of filling it with children. This isn't the way we thought we would do it, but I know God has a plan and these children are part of it. I know we will love them all as dearly as if they were conceived in a more traditional way."

A commotion in the door yead alerted them to the return of James and the other men. He prayed the grizzly scene his son encountered at the Indian village had not scarred him for life.

"The bodies are buried." James said, once he washed up and joined them in the parlor. "I didn't know anyone could be so cruel as to massacre an entire village of innocent people. The strange thing was there were no young braves or men among the dead. They were all older people, women and children."

"I should have studied the scene more closely when I was there," Caleb confessed. "I didn't realize the absence of the young men."

"We didn't either, at first sight, but as we worked with the dead bodies we came to that realization.

"Are you all right, James?" Caleb asked, as he studied the sadness mirrored in his son's blue eyes.

"I'm appalled and angry. It will take a long time for the vision of what I saw today to leave my mind. There were several maidens I got to know over the years and hoped to take one of them as my wife then the time was right. Now it will never be right."

Caleb ached to think the time for James' desire would never come to fruition. At the age of seventeen, Caleb was in love with a young lass from the village, but because he never made his feelings known, his older brother, Eric, took her has his bride. Being the younger brother, he had no say in the matter. Instead, he learned the craft of horse breeding and as soon as he could he left for the new world. Had he married his first love, he wouldn't have met Maude and gained a son any man would be proud to call his own.

Maude was quick to change the subject from death and unrequited love to that of dinner.

During his conversation with James, Elizabeth took Ella into one of the bedrooms and helped her dry her hair, and dress in a fashionable gown that Elizabeth had outgrown.

"The dress is a little tight in the bust, but I can fix that later," Elizabeth said. "I can smell something good cooking in the kitchen. I'm hungry and so is Ella."

Supper was, as usual, delicious and nutritious. What bothered Caleb most was when Ella seated herself cross-legged on the floor.

"Why aren't you sitting at the table with the rest of the family?" James asked.

"In my village, this is how we sit to eat. Master Shamas always threw my food on the floor."

James reached out his hand to Ella. "You're part of this family now. We all sit at the table and tonight you are an honored guest. Without you, my new son and your daughter would have to go hungry. I think I speak for our entire family when I say we are all pleased with not only the babies but also for you becoming another sister."

Ella got to her feet and took her place at the table. Before they began to eat, Caleb raised his voice in prayer. "Dear Lord, thank you for this nourishing meal the three new family members who have joined us today. We are blessed with the bounty you have given us, on this day of sorrow, rebirth, and freedom. Amen."

With supper finished, the early dusk of the spring evening started spreading across the farm. From his pocket, he produced his pipe and tamped it with the tobacco grown in the area. It was something Hunting Hawk gave him, and he always thanked his friend when he took the first pull of smoke into his body.

He sensed the presence of someone, long before sight or sound alerted him to the man who stepped from the shadows of the wooded area boarding the south side of his farm.

"Greetings my friend," Hunting Hawk's deep accented voice cut into the night.

"My son said there were no men or young braves among the dead. How did you know where to come?'

"My men and the young braves were on the first hunt of the year. It was The Old One who told us what happened. She was up early and went to relieve herself. When the attack began, she hid and watched the carnage. She was about to return to the village when you came and helped with the birth of my child. She remained hidden until after your men finished burring the dead to save them from the scavengers that had begun to gather. I am forever in debt to you for your kindness."

"Have you come for your son?" Caleb inquired.

Saying the words tore at his heart. He came to love the boy as his own. To have him taken away would be devastating for the entire family.

"He is too small to follow me. We have found refuge in the village of The Old One's birth. Knowing he is well cared for is enough for me. From time to time, I will leave game for your table and ask only that the boy not forget who his father is. When he is old enough, I will make myself know to him. Have you given him a name."

Caleb nodded. "We plan to call him Matthew Hawk. In that way we will honor not only his father but also mine."

"You are a good man, Caleb, and a loyal friend. Your name will be honored by my people for many generations to come. For now, I need to establish myself in my new village and to mourn the loss of my life mate. Take care of my son and love him as your own. We will meet again as our lives will always be intertwined."

Hunting Hawk melted back into the darkness of the forest and disappeared. In his place, the carcass of a freshly killed dear hung to cure. They would enjoy many meals from his precious gift. Although the meat was appreciated, nothing could compare to the son Hunting Hawk trusted him to raise as his own.

Chapter Two
Fourteen years later

Becky Hilman couldn't believe what her father just told her. "What do you mean we're moving to the frontier? I-I don't want to leave Philadelphia."

"We have no choice. You know your Uncle Richard never liked me. He always thought your mother married beneath her station in life. It's either move to the frontier and start a new store or be homeless here. I don't prefer the latter, so I've agreed. Without the position her father's put me in I must establish a store wherever your uncle tells me to go."

"I could stay here and live with Uncle Richard and Aunt Mary."

"What would you plan to do here? You're only fourteen years old. The man I met with, Dr. James MacAfee, came to your uncle with the proposition of the new store. It's an opportunity neither of us can afford to turn down."

Becky lowered her eyes. She didn't want to talk further with her father. He hadn't done well when her mother died of pneumonia a year ago. Instead of properly running the store, he'd begun to drink and became abusive to her. Maybe a new start was what they needed. Her father was right. With his reputation in Philadelphia, it was enough for any potential suitor to stay away from her door. There was nothing left here. Even Uncle Richard and Aunt Mary were more aloof with each passing day.

"I'll start packing for the journey, Father. How much of the furniture are we bringing with us."

"None of the large pieces as they will be too bulky to transport. We should be able to sell them for a good price as they are all quality items. We will need the money."

"Mama left her special furniture to me. I insist the money be put in an account in my name. I won't have you spending it on whiskey. You can have the profits from the store, but the money from Mama's furniture is mine."

"You are a child. What do you know of finances?"

"I am the one who has been keeping the books for the store ever since before Mama got sick. She said I should know about such things. I know you are making money, but you are spending it on whiskey and women. I will not have you squander Mama's inheritance in such horrible ways. If we are making a new start, I will do it with my own funds."

William Hillman hung his head. Becky knew he understood what she was telling him. Maybe the move to the frontier would be a new beginning for them.

~ * ~

"I still can't believe you were able to get a shopkeeper to open a store in the area," Caleb said as he pounded the last nail into the new general store, with the living quarters on the upper floor.

"I've always known we needed a store closer than the one we've been going to," James replied. "While I was in Philadelphia, taking Sophie as my bride, I told her about the situation here. She said she knew someone who owns two stores in Philadelphia and was willing to close one of the stores and relocate here. The man who will be coming is the brother-in-law of the owner. His name is William Hillman, and he has a fourteen-year-old daughter. I think they said her name is Becky."

The mention of a fourteen-year-old daughter reminded him of his children. Matt, who now wished to be called Hawk, and Susan just recently turned fourteen. Ella was in the process of opening a restaurant in the new settlement, where the general store was to be located and Elizabeth recently married Tomas Hanson, the new minister who permanently settled not far from the centger of a;; the new businesses that were being opened.

The area was growing and mostly because of the wealth provided by the quality horses Caleb bred and sold to wealthy men as far away as Boston.

Even Hawk was comfortable with his lifestyle. He loved working with horses and often went to be with Hunting Hawk. It was good he was able to learn of his heritage not only within Caleb's household, but that of the people of his birth.

The sound of horse harnesses broke into Caleb's private thoughts. Looking up, he saw several wagons approaching them.

"It looks like Mr. Hillman and the supplies for the store have arrived," James observed. "Maybe we should send someone out to the farm to get some men to help the teamsters unload them."

"That's a good idea. In the meantime, it's getting too late to get them settled tonight. I know your mother and the girls will be more than willing to put them up at the house tonight. We'll send someone over and have Ella and Elizabeth go out there to help."

Caleb watched as William Hillman jumped down from the seat of the wagon he'd been driving. Rather than help his daughter get down, he hurried over to James and Caleb.

"You must be Caleb MacAfee," he said extending his hand in greeting. "I've had the pleasure of meeting Dr. MacAfee when he was in Philadelphia."

Ignoring the obvious snub, James went to the wagon where Becky was seated.

Caleb smiled with pride to see his son playing the gentleman, when the girl's father left her to her own devices.

"The hour is late," Caleb said. "We've sent a message to my daughters. Elizabeth and Ella, as well as James' wife to go out to the farm, so my wife and children can arrange for you to spend the night. Tomorrow we'll return here and help you get settled. In the meantime, my men will help the teamsters unload the wagons so they can go back to Philadelphia when they finish."

"That's very generous of you, Mr. MacAfee, but I'm certain my daughter is capable of getting our passions settled, if you'll show us where the house is located."

"There is no house. Your accommodation is in the apartment on the top floor of the store. I doubt if she would be able to settle things by herself. In the morning, my sons and my employees will come and help with the arrangement of the furnishings. Now, if you don't mind riding in James' carriage, we'll go out to the farm. By the time we get there, I'm certain my wife and daughter will have supper ready."

"As I said before, Becky can settle our belongings. There is no need to further inconvenience you. I'm certain your men have other tasks they should be handling."

Caleb wanted to say something, but he remained silent. Somehow, the man expected a grand house as well as God only knew what else. He was going to be someone who would prove difficult to deal with on a regular basis.

~ * ~

Maude left Susan in the kitchen, while she put fresh bedding in the rooms vacated by James, Elizabeth and Ella when they went out on their own. She was so proud of all her children. Hawk and Susan were the only ones of her brood left at home. Hawk was a great help with the horses, when he wasn't with Hunting Hawk. Since the massacre, there had been no more violence between the local villages and the white community.

Someone knocked at the door, but before she could answer it, Hawk took over the duties of man of the house.

"What do you want here?" she heard Hawk ask.

"I've come for what is mine. I want my daughter."

Maude picked up the long gun from the bedroom she shared with Caleb. Once in the foyer, she saw Shames standing toe to toe with Hawk.

"You won't touch my sister," Hark said.

Maude could tell he was holding in his temper.

"She's not your sister. The brat, as well as her mother, are my property. They have become beautiful women and will bring a good price in the slave market."

"The way I see it," Maude declared, "you will be taking up residence in the graveyard if you don't get off our property. Ella and Susan are as much our children as our other children are."

"I know for a fact James is the son of your dead first husband, and this savage is from that Indian village we wiped out. It's too bad Caleb didn't come along later than he did. That way the brat would have died before he had a chance to live."

Enraged, Maude raised the long gun, closed her eyes and fired a shot. It was true that Caleb taught her how to use the gun, but she'd never fired it at a living being, be it man or beast, before.

Shamas yelped in pain and ran back to where his horse was tied, leaving a trail of blood in his wake. He was not out of the dooryard when Caleb rode in.

~ * ~

Caleb heard the report of gunfire just as he approached the door yard of the farm. The scene in front of him made his blood run cold. Maude stood in the doorway, his long gun on the floor beside her, as she stepped back from the force of the gun going off. In front of his wife, Shamas held his ear, which was bleeding profusely.

"What's going on here?" Caleb demanded.

"That bitch, you call your wife, tried to kill me."

"That's not right, Pa," Hawk insisted. "He came here and wanted to take Susan to the slave market. Ma heard him talking to me and came out with the long gun. She didn't intend to kill him. He said some terrible things, and she tried to scare him off. She shot and the bullet hit his ear. If I'd been the one with the gun, he wouldn't have gotten off so easily."

"Is that true?" Caleb demanded.

"The girl belongs to me. I'm her father and I could use the money she would bring at the slave market."

"She doesn't belong to you. As I recall, fourteen years ago I paid you handsomely for both Susan and Ella. I have their freedom papers, and they have been raised as our daughters, with the love they deserve."

"He told Me he was with the men who killed everyone in the village of my birth. He murdered the people. He even said he wished you'd arrived later, and I would have died. He called me a savage."

"Do you believe this liar over me?" Shamas asked.

"I'd believe a snake over you. I want you out of the old settlement before the end of the week. That's when I will be going to the county seat and report everything to the constable. I will also ask him to investigate the disappearance of your wife, Susan. Do you know our daughter is named for her because of the kindness she showed Ella? Of course, if you don't leave the settlement, I will turn you over to Hunting Hawk and his people."

"Slaves don't deserve names," Shamas said as though he hadn't heard the statement about Hunting Hawk's people.

"All living beings deserve names. Even my horses are named. As for you, I will make sure the remainder of your life is a living hell if you are still in the old settlement past my deadline. Now, I want you off my property and don't even think about approaching either Ella or Susan again. If you do, I will finish what my wife started and there isn't a jury in the world who would convict me for protecting my family."

For emphasis, Caleb pulled his gun, prompting Shamas to ride away as though the hounds of hell were chasing him.

Rather than waiting for the Hillson's to arrive, Caleb hurried to the house to see to his wife. "James is on his way," he reassured Maude, as he helped to take a seat on the setae. "Did he hurt you?"

"Not physically. He said terrible things and threatened the children. I was so frightened. I only shot the gun to scare him off. I didn't…" she dissolved in tears before she could finish what she was saying.

Caleb was relieved when James entered the house to take over the care of his mother. While he assessed the damage done by the recoil of the gun, Caleb relayed the information of what went on while they were at the new settlement.

"Do you think he'll leave?" James asked.

"He will if he knows what's good for him. I told him if he wasn't gone by the end of the week, I would be going to the constable and report what he told your mother and Hawk about the massacre in the Indian village, along with the disappearance of his wife, Susan. I also threatened to turn him over to Hunting Hawk. I know his people would like nothing more than retribution for the evil they did during the massacre."

James smiled. "When you put the fear of God into someone, Pa, you do it in style. Since I've been in my private practice, I made some inquiries about the lady in question. He didn't kill her, but he tried. It seems he beat her for caring for Ella. That night, she ran away from him. Friends in the next village over helped her to get to Boston. Once she was there. She contacted a lawyer and put her husband aside. They told me she is remarried and is very happy."

"Does Shamas know this?"

"If he does, he doesn't talk about it. I think that the nasty whiskey he drinks at the tavern has blurred his memory. I tell my patients, if they want to have a drink, they do it in more reputable places."

Caleb had no time to bask in his pride for his son for looking into something so far in the past, as the Hillson's along with Ella and Elizabeth arrived at the farm.

"We heard a shot," William began, "then on the way in, we saw a man riding away and bleeding."

"It was a personal dispute between one of the less reputable men in the old settlement. You won't have to worry about him in the future, as he isn't allowed to set foot in the new settlement. He's also been advised to leave the area and not come back. My wife shot to scare him, not to wound him, in defense of our family. Now, from the smell coming from the kitchen, I am certain Susan has supper well underway for you. Once you've eaten, we will get you settled in your rooms. I'm certain Becky will be comfortable sleeping in a soft bed tonight."

Caleb led the way to the dining room where Maude already sat with her arm in a sling.

"How badly is she hurt?" he asked.

"Not bad, Pa, but I thought it best she rests her arm while it heals. The sling is for support, nothing more. Ella and Elizabeth are willing to spend the night. Elizabeth's husband, Tom, will be joining us soon. I'm certain we can all use his prayers. Since it's Monday he won't be having a service until next Sunday. His partitioners will understand, when they learn what went on here this afternoon."

Once they seated themselves at the table, Ella and Susan brought out platters of steaming food, including a succulent venison roast, winter vegetables, and flaky rolls,

"Everything looks delicious," William declared.

His appreciation faded when Susan and Ella took their seats at the table. "Do you allow your slaves to eat at your table."

"There are no slaves in this household. Ella and Susan are free women and our daughters. I rescued Ella and Susan from a cruel master, just months after Susan was born. That man was the one you saw leaving here when you arrived. I gave them both their freedom as soon as I was able to get to the county seat and file the papers. I'll thank you to treat them with the respect they deserve."

"What about him?" William inquired, pointing his finger at Hawk.

"Hawk is also our son. We have raised him since the day he was born. His given name is Matthew Hawk, but he prefers to be called Hawk in honor of the people he lost in the massacre. It's a long story and one not suitable for the conversation while we partake of the supper Susan has prepared."

Elizabeth's husband, Thomas, arrived, changing the demeanor of the room. "I'm sorry if I'm late. I was sitting with a sick parishioner. I'm afraid his days on this earth are numbered."

"I know who you mean. I've done all that I can do," James replied. "His fate is in God's hands now."

"You're just in time to say grace, Thomas," Caleb said, once the formal introductions between Tom and the Hillman's were made.

"Dear Heavenly Father, thank you for the bounty of this table and the hands that prepared it. Thank you for bringing William Hillman and his daughter safely into our midst. Help them to become revered members of our new settlement. Amen."

Caleb watched as William beamed at the mention of his name in the prayer. It was also evident the man chafed at the presence of Ella and Susan at the table.

"My compliments, Mrs. MacAfee," William gushed. "This is some of the best beef I've ever eaten."

"I don't deserve your praises. Susan is becoming as accomplished a cook as Ella is. When she is older, she wants to move to the settlement and work in the restaurant Ella has established. It is becoming so busy, Ella will soon not be able to handle it alone. I don't know what I will do without her."

William made no response. Caleb wondered what the man would think if he knew the meat was venison and not beef. It was no wonder his brother-in-law was anxious to send him to the frontier.

With supper ended, the girls began to clean up the kitchen. It came as a surprise when Becky joined them.

"My daughter isn't used to dealing with…"

"Your daughter is a delightful young lady. As for your accommodation for the night, you will be sleeping in James' old bedroom and Becky will be given the room where Elizabeth and Ella grew up."

"What about him?"

"When the weather is warm, Hawk prefers to sleep in a tent in the backyard. He enjoys being outdoors."

"How do I know your little savage won't sneak back into the house and rape my daughter. I would be more comfortable with Becky bunking in with me."

"I'm not comfortable with you sharing a room with your daughter. She deserves her own room and while she is under my roof, she will be treated with the greatest respect. As for Hawk sneaking back into the house, it will not happen. As I said before, when the weather is mild, he prefers to sleep in his tent. I'm certain you remember when you were fourteen years old and turning into a young man. He wants to do his own thing, and we are proud of his honesty to say nothing of his maturity. One day, he will run this farm and raise the quality horses that we are known for."

Without further comment, William filled his pipe and took a long draw. There would be no more conversation this evening. At least the man's silence came as a relief to Caleb.

Chapter Three

A good night's sleep didn't seem to mellow William's disposition. He was fully dressed when he came to the breakfast table. He hardly looked like a man who was ready to settle into his new store to say nothing of the living accommodations on the second floor of the building.

"I assume the teamsters I hired in Philadelphia have already begun to settle us into our new home. It certainly isn't the grand house I expected, although I am certain Becky and I will be able to make do until something more suitable has been erected."

"Would you like for me to find one of the girls from the settlement to help Becky with the cooking and cleaning?" Ella inquired.

"I don't think that will be necessary. I plan to visit the slave market and buy a girl for that. I won't have to pay her on a weekly basis and I'm certain she will be able to handle any other thing I need for her to do for me."

Caleb watched as Ella chafed at his suggestion. More than anyone else at the table, she understood what he was implying.

"We did the best we could with the time we had," Caleb replied.

As soon as they finished breakfast, Thomas took William and Becky back to the new settlement. "I don't like that man," Caleb said to Maude. "He reminds me of Shamas. Since James knows the brother-in-law, I'm going to have him send a letter asking how to handle the situation."

"That's a good suggestion, but I worry about his daughter. I wonder how he treats her when no one else is around. I'm afraid he has subjected her to abuse. The very fact he wanted her to sleep in his room makes me nervous. I wonder what he did to her on their journey here. To be honest he scares me."

"He scares me, too," Hawk interjected. "If I thought the people in the old settlement were cruel, they can't hold a candle to the way that man looked at me. It was enough to send chills through my body."

"I have a feeling he is abusive to his daughter. If it wasn't for her, I would never step foot in his store."

Caleb watched as his son nodded in agreement. It was evident Becky Hillman entranced Hawk the minute he first saw her. It was the same way he felt about Maude from the minute they met.

"When my chores are finished may I have permission to go into the settlement and help them settle the store and living quarters?"

"After the way that man treated you, are you certain you want to help him?"

"Not him, Becky. I doubt he will lift a finger to help her settle things. To be truthful, I doubt he will be here long enough to establish the store. I know we need the store. I also know it will be up to Becky to run it. Hopefully, when James contacts the true owner of the establishment, he will be able to do something to make Becky a success."

~ * ~

"Ella MacAfee is right, Papa," Becky said once they stood in the newly built store surrounded by unopened boxes. "If you buy a bed slave, you will have to support her for the rest of her life. She will be expected to cook and clean in addition to gracing your bed. I'm not comfortable with slavery. We can hire a girl from town to teach me to cook. I already know how to clean a house, and I know I can run the store. I've been keeping the books ever since Mama died. What I won't do is grace your bed."

"What about me? I have needs. We need a slave."

"Maybe you do, but I need a father. I've always known you desired a son when I was born. Nothing I've ever done is good enough. We decided this venture will be a new start for us. Well, my start is now. If you won't be a man and do the things that need doing, you can go back to Philadelphia. I'm certain one of the ladies who you have been with every night will welcome you. The choice is yours."

"What do you know…?"

"More than you think. Like I say, the choice is yours. Uncle Richard warned me about your activities. I may not be fully grown, but I've had to grow up quickly since Mama died. When you were out with your lady friends, Uncle Richard was training me to run the store. He trusts me, a child, more than he does you."

"Damn your mother and that brother of hers."

He raised his hand to strike her, but Becky was faster than him dodging the blow he hoped to inflict on her. Instead of flesh connecting with flesh, his hand only felt air.

Becky turned her back on him and stormed further into the store. She'd been taught to be an independent woman over the past year, and she wouldn't allow her father to take that independence away from her. He could rot in hell for all she cared. Hopefully she'd made an impression on him, and he would change his ways. If he didn't, she would have to cross that bridge when she came to it.

For now, she needed to unpack the inventory for the store and get ready to do business. As for the upstairs apartment, she could spread quilts on the floor until she was able to figure out how to arrange the furniture the teamsters took to the apartment before they left to return to Philadelphia.

She no more than started unpacking when Hawk arrived at the store.

"I came here to see if I could help you with the unpacking. I don't see your father anywhere, so I know he's not helping you. Just point me as where to put the inventory once it's unpacked."

"I know you probably have chores to do at the farm, but I do appreciate your help."

Her appreciation was met with a brilliant smile. With his black hair, brown eyes and coppery skin, she thought he was one of the most handsome young men she'd ever met.

Each box she opened reminded her of the Christmas presents her mother piled beneath the Christmas catus for her to open. The quality of the merchandise her uncle sent to stock the shelves rivaled anything the stores in Philadelphia carried in their inventory.

By the time Hawk left to ride back to the farm, about half of the boxes were empty. Without his help, she would never have been able to make such good progress on her own.

Her father left right after their confrontation and did not return until late that evening. When he did return, he reeked of cheap alcohol.

"Where am I to sleep tonight?" he bellowed when he entered the still unsettled apartment.

"On the floor like me. While you were sitting at the tavern wasting money, I was stocking the store. It was a blessing that Hawk came to help me with the unpacking and stocking of the shelves. It is important to get it up and running."

"There's no food on the stove. What am I to eat?"

"I'm certain you will be able to find something among the supplies in the store. As for me, I was blessed to have Ella bring me my noon and evening meals."

William went down to the lower level of the building and Becky returned to writing the letter to her uncle. She'd been composing it in her head ever since the confrontation with her father. Something needed to be done and done quickly. This was her new beginning, and she didn't deserve the actions of her father to ruin it for her.

Not caring if her father came to the upstairs apartment, Becky gave into the exhaustion from the day spent store. With luck she would be able to open for business within the week. Once she was running the new store, she could consider settling the apartment. She knew her father would be of no help in either venture.

~ * ~

Nothing about this new venture was going as William planned. The store wasn't one of the elegant businesses he was used to working at in Philadelphia. There had been no home for them other than an upstairs apartment and Caleb MacAfee acted like they should be in their debt for what they'd built. As for Becky, she'd gone from a sweet young lady who studied hard and sat primly with her embroidery to a carbon copy of her overbearing mother.

Her comment about having help from Hawk rubbed him the wrong way. He certainly didn't want the little savage sniffing around his daughter.

Even though Richard negotiated a good price for his dead wife's furniture, none of the money was put in his hand. The man had the money into an account only Becky could obtain. She was underage, for god's sake. As his daughter, he deserved that money. Instead, Richard sent him only a small salary to see to his needs.

It would serve Becky right if I just disappeared. The only problem is money. I need to figure out how to get my hands on her inheritance before I go back north. There's nothing for me in Philadelphia. Maybe I'll go to Boston. No one knows me there. I could get a good position that pays more than I'll ever get from Richard.

Chapter Four

Richard Peters held the two letters that arrived within days of each other. The first one came from Dr. MacAfee voicing his concerns about William and his actions since arriving in the new settlement. From the date on the letter, it was written the day after William and Becky were scheduled to arrive.

The second letter was posted a day later, and it came from Becky. When his niece and brother-in-law lived in Philadelphia, Richard had no idea of the abuse Becky suffered at the hands of her father. It was true William was certainly no businessman. That was the reason Richard insisted Becky learn how to run the store and keep the books.

These new accusations raised his ire. He was going to have to find a way to investigate the situation and decide how to handle it.

"Mary. We need to talk."

Mary Peters was a petite woman in her late thirties. They'd never been able to have children, so Becky had become very special to her, especially after the death of his sister, Amy.

"Does it have anything to do with the posts you received?"

"Yes, it does. You are very perceptive. Things are not well with Becky and William. I gave that man the opportunity of a lifetime and he has already alienated the residents of the new settlement and the outlying farms. Becky also wrote and detailed the abuse she has experienced both in the new settlement and here in Philadelphia. I need to hire a coach and go out there myself to straighten things out."

"I'm going with you," Mary declared. "Against my better judgement, I backed off, in the hopes of Becky and William learning to work together. I will not allow her to face this alone. Do they have accommodations for us?"

"In the letter I received from Dr. MacAfee, he said his parents have enough room to accommodate visitors. The elder MacAfee is very concerned about William's attitude and Becky's safety. We need to leave post haste. I'm afraid William will, in one of his drunken sprees, do harm to Becky to take control of her inheritance."

~ * ~

Becky never felt so alone in her life. She'd been in the new settlement for several weeks and still hadn't found the time to settle the upstairs apartment. She'd hoped her father would take on that job, but it hadn't happened.

She saw him in the morning when he went to the restaurant for his breakfast, He would return at noon with the dinner that was to last her for dinner and supper for that day. Otherwise, when he was in the store, he flirted with the women who came into shop. It didn't matter if they were married or single, he would shower them with compliments.

Becky knew he was hoping one of them would invite him into her bed, since he disliked sleeping on the makeshift pallet on the bedroom floor.

Earlier in the day, she'd been surprised when Hawk came and offered to set up the furniture she hadn't had time to put in their proper places. Unfortunately, William ordered him to leave. The one light of hope for becoming settled dimed quickly.

She turned her thoughts to the aunt and uncle she'd left behind in Philadelphia. She thought they loved her, but the letter she'd written just after her arrival went unanswered. She was alone on the frontier with the father who wanted only to abuse her. She gave thanks that his evenings were spent at the tavern in the old settlement. Only once had he tried to climb in her bed on a night when the alcohol took over his senses. A perfectly placed knee to his groin forced him back to his own pallet.

The bell over the door of the store jangled, signaling the arrival of a customer. With William at the restaurant ordering their noon meal, Becky hurried to greet the people who just entered the store. From the footsteps, she knew there were at least two, she was excited to be of assistance to them.

"Uncle Richard, Aunt Mary, what are you doing here?"

"I received the letter you sent, along with one from Dr. MacAfee. He is concerned with William's behavior as well as your safety. As soon as I read the letters, I knew I needed to come and investigate things for myself. I will not have my name associated with the behavior of your father. In the short time he has been here, he had made several enemies."

Becky felt her heart sink. She'd worked hard to get the store ready for customers to come in. Slowly, the members of the community were coming to shop, even though they would only deal with her, she felt as though she was making progress.

"Don't cry," Mary implored. "You have done a wonderful job with the store. We met with Dr. MacAfee, and he sang your praises. We've come to see what we can do to help you."

"But I have no place for you to stay."

"Accommodations have been made for us to stay at the MacAfee farm. The people here hold you in high esteem. It is a shame that the same thing cannot be said for your father. In a short time, there is bad blood between him and the members of this community. William needs to account for his behavior."

"Did I hear my name?" William said, as he entered the store carrying a tray of food. He stopped short, when he saw Richard and Mary were the people talking to his daughter.

"What are you doing here?"

"We have received letters detailing your behavior since arriving here," Richard said. "I've learned not only have you been acting like you are better than the hard-working people you were sent here to serve, but also the abusive behavior you've been subjecting Becky to."

"Who would spread such lies?"

"Who do you think, Papa. It's time the truth is known. I said nothing about it when we were in Philadelphia, because I was afraid no one would believe a child. I'm no longer a child. You have seen to that, since we arrived here. You have left all the responsibilities of setting up and running the store to me. It is as though you think such tasks are beneath you. You are more interested in talking to the women who come in to shop and drinking your nights away than you are in helping me with anything. You complain about not having a bed to sleep in, but I have not seen you try to settle the apartment. Just today, Hawk was in to offer his help with our living area, and you insulted him. You told him that savages are not allowed to come to the store."

"I was within my rights. Everyone knows the Indians will steal you blind if you give them a chance. I won't have him taking what is mine."

"Nothing here is yours, William," Richard replied. "I have put the store and all the furnishings in Becky's name. What you don't know is that I've been here for several days. I've spoken with the families both in town and the surrounding farms. You have no place here, William. Mary and I are prepared to stay until competent help can be found to lighten Becky's load. As for you, I'm giving you until tomorrow morning to pack your things and leave here. Had I known what was going on in your household, I would have never moved Becky out here. As things stand, I've learned that here, my niece has become a respected businesswoman. She deals with the customers fairly and with the respect they deserve. With the proper assistance, she will do well."

"Wh-where will I go?" William stammered.

"I don't care, but don't think you can ever use my name as a reference or even acknowledge you know me. You are dead to me. The only good thing to come from your union with my sister is Becky. She has her mother's brilliant mind and determination. Unlike you, she has a fine work ethic. Mary and I are extremely proud of her. Now, I think you have some packing to do. I have purchased a horse from Caleb MacAfee for you to have the means to leave and never return."

Becky watched as her uncle handed her father an envelope. She wondered what it contained. What else would he be willing to give his former brother-in-law?

"This envelope contains enough money for you to make a new start. The money and the horse are not a gift, but a means to get you out of Becky's life."

Before her eyes, Becky saw her father melt into a tantrum, not unlike one a toddler would throw to get his own way. No matter how much her father railed about how unfair Richard was being, her uncle stood his ground. Veiled threats were made on both sides, until at last, William retreated to the upstairs apartment and started packing.

It wasn't long before William reappeared carrying a small valise. "You'll regret this, Richard." He yelled as he made his way toward the front door. "I'll leave and your precious store will fail. I don't know how you can entrust such an undertaking to a child. Mark my words, within the year, she will be back in Philadelphia with her tail between her legs. When she does, what will she have to look forward to? She's not suited to be a rich man's servant, and she will end up becoming a whore. That's all that women are put upon the earth to do."

Without even a word of farewell to Becky, he left the store and mounted the horse that stood patiently waiting for him.

"He's full of bust and bluster, Becky. Had I known of his abuse to you, I would have intervened and brought you to our home to live. I am so sorry I didn't see the signs of what he was doing to you. Here your future is a bright one and I will move heaven and earth, to secure your success."

Chapter Five

As the years passed, the settlement grew into a proper village. Caleb was proud of the accomplishments of the people who came to build up the area.

Ella's restaurant drew happy customers and grew to the point where Susan would drive into the village daily to work with her mother. Love had also come to the restaurant when a free black man came to town with the ambition of opening a proper blacksmith shop for the neighboring farmers. It didn't take long before Simon Bartle came to the MacAfee farm to ask for Ella's hand in marriage.

Caleb was pleased with the man who now ran a prospering business during the day and supported Ella's dreams at night. He couldn't hope for a harder working man to call his son-in-law.

It wasn't long before Ella and Simon were expecting their first child.

James' practice grew along with his family. He and Sophie were parents of a boy and a girl. New life was making its way into the village. With James' growing practice and family, Maude now came into town three days a week to give Sophie a needed break from her duties in the doctor's office and as a mother.

Although Hawk now ran the farm with the efficiency that matched Caleb's love of the land and the horses, he had suffered a loss, when Hunting Hawk was killed in a skirmish with an invading tribe. They were conquered easily, but with the loss of their best hunter, the people became aloof where Hawk was concerned.

As a young man, Hawk took the snub in his stride and poured his heart and energy into the farm. Caleb knew it was his son's hope that he would be able to take Becky Hillman as his wife. Unfortunately, she was a beautiful girl and attracted the attention of many of the new residences moving into the area. Hawk still thought of the days when the people from the old settlement called him Savage.

Putting aside his thoughts of their children, Caleb made his way to his son's office. Today was one of the days when Maude helped in the office, while Sophie cared for the children and prepared the supper he and Maude would enjoy.

"Pa, it's good to see you," James greeted him. "I've closed the office for the day, and Sophie and Ma are busy in the kitchen. Until they are ready for us to eat, I have something to talk to you about."

Caleb was intrigued. What could James possibly have to say that couldn't be discussed in front of the women and children?

"You look worried. Is something wrong? Do you have an ill patient that is on your mind."

"It's not that. I received a letter from Sophie's brother, Paul, today. There is talk about war with the British rumbling in Philadelphia. There is even a rumor that the lads who are pushing for this war dumped a load of tea in Boston harbor. Just recently, Paul met with a young surveyor named Geore Washington, and they talked about independence for the states."

"Independence," Caleb repeated. "I'm surprised something like this hasn't happened before this."

"If war is to come, what side will you take?"

"I'm a Scotsman, James. My family has been fighting the English for more generations than I care to count. My sympathies are with the freedom fighters. If I were younger, I would consider fighting, but this is a young man's war. It will be up to young men like Hawk to make their decision and fight for whichever side they choose. If nothing else, I can support the cause in different ways, be it financially or with horses."

"I was hoping that would be your answer. I will be aligning myself with the freedom fighters, should war come to fruition. I've spoken of this with Simon and Thomas, and they agree with the idea of freedom for the colonies. I've yet to speak with Hawk about it."

"What of your practice, your patients?"

"Although Sophie doesn't have the formal education that I do, I have trained her and leaned heavily on her for help with my practice. All will be well where they are concerned.

Caleb nodded. His son was a practical man who would not allow the people of the village to suffer in his absence.

"I still need to know where Hawk's sympathies are," James said changing the subject back to what was lying the most heavily on his mind.

"I know where Hawk will stand. Before the British came, this land belonged to his people and the other peaceful tribes in the area. They have often butted heads with the ruling government. It would be ideal if he could persuade the tribes to join us. Unfortunately, his relationship with his father's people has deteriorated since Hunting Hawk was killed during a skirmish with a warring tribe. That man was the link between tribe and us. The fact Hawk was raised in a white household has alienated their loyalty to him. Only time will tell if they are willing to support war if it does come."

~ * ~

Hawk was reluctant to return to his father's people, but with the rumblings of war, he needed to see if they would be willing to fight on their own terms against the British who treated them as one step above the animals.

~ * ~

Becky prospered to grow the store to rival the one her Uncle Richard ran in Philadelphia. Ever since the day her father took the horse and money from her uncle, she'd heard not word one from the man. His silence came as no surprise. She didn't care if he was dead or alive.

When she received the letter from her uncle saying there were rumblings of war circulating in Philadelphia, she wondered what side her uncle would take. She knew if her father was alive, he would be siding with the British. She decided it would be best if she kept her opinions to herself and see what was coming.

More than anything else, she wanted to marry Hawk. She saw him in church every Sunday, but she was too shy to take the first step. She'd heard rumors of how people treated him. Even the prominence of Caleb MacAfee, the stigma of him being born to Indian parents followed him throughout the village.

With the thought of war, she wondered what it would mean for the young man who stole her heart the first time she saw him. If he went to fight the British, it was possible he might not return to the village. Perhaps the time was right for her to make her feelings known.

As though Hawk read her mind, he entered the store. "Good afternoon, Miss Becky," he said as soon as he approached her. "I need some supplies. Since Ma and Pa are eating supper with James and Sophie tonight, I was wondering if you would be willing to accompany me to the restaurant. Ella has agreed to prepare a meal especially for us, even though the restaurant is closed."

Becky smiled. He'd never made such an invitation before. "I would be pleased to go to the restaurant with you. Stephen is capable of handling things at the store."

Silently, she thanked her uncle for sending Steven Cartridge from Philadelphia to work in the store. At one point, he'd suggested they should become a couple, but she told him no. He was her employee and if that wasn't enough for him, he could go back to Philadelphia and look for work there.

He made the decision to stay and retained his residence at the boarding house that an older widow ran on the other side of the village. In return, he'd become a valued employee and courted one of the farm girls from the area. It wouldn't be long before they would be getting married and building a home of their own close to the store.

While Hawk chose his purchases, Becky told Stephen of her plans for the evening. He assured her he would finish the necessary duties and close the store. With a sly wink, he told her to have a good time.

After removing her shopkeeper's apron, she pinched her cheeks and ran her tongue over her lips to moisten them before walking across the street to the restaurant, where they would be having the evening meal.

Becky always marveled at the quality of the tables and chairs that Hawk and his father fashioned for Ella's establishment. In the few years it had been open, the restaurant doubled in size, making room for more patrons.

Susan greeted them as soon as they entered. "I'm pleased to see you here, my brother. Since I know what pried you away from the farm please take a seat anywhere in the restaurant."

Hawk gave her a wide smile. "What special meal are you and Ella serving tonight?"

"Beef stew, freshly made bread and cake for dessert."

"That sounds delicious," Becky said.

Once their order was taken, Hawk reached across the table and took Becky's hand. "Until today I've been a coward. I have admired you from afar, but I didn't think I was good enough for you

Becky opened her mouth, wanting to say how much she wanted him to notice her.

"Please let me finish. My father and brother have spoken to me about the possibility of war."

"I know. I received a letter from my uncle today saying Philadelphia is in turmoil over it."

"If it comes, I'll be going away for a while. I'm going to fight, but in my own way. I will go to my father's people and tell them what is happening. Ever since he was killed, I have not been welcomed in their village. That will be spoken of and hopefully rectified. Should the war come, I will be aligning with them. I want to fight the British, but not in the traditional way. The people have been mistreated by the British, ever since they invaded the land of our ancestors. For years I have been called a savage and perhaps everyone is right. I will fight for what is right, just not the same as the others. I didn't want to leave without telling you of my feelings for you. If I return after the war, I want you to be my wife."

Becky broke into a wide grin. "There is nothing I want more than to be married to you. When the time comes to make our decision known, I will contact my uncle and let him know of our intentions. I will be worried sick if you leave the area, but a man must do what he feels is right."

"I was hoping that would be your reaction."

"What of your father and brother? Will they fight."

"Father wants to, but he told James this is a young man's war to fight. He wants Father to stay here, run the farm and protect the women. As for James, Thomas and Simon, they are prepared to do what must be done to gain freedom from England. The army will need medical attention as well as someone to see to their spiritual needs. As a free black man, Simon has the strength and determination to fight for what he feels is right. Should the need arise, the girls will be moving back to the farm to be under Father and Mother's protection. What will you do?"

"The store must stay open. I am certain Stephen will be willing to fight as well. I will take in his wife and together we will weather whatever storm should come our way."

From the look on Hawk's face, she knew he didn't approve of her decision, but he accepted it. The tension she'd felt with the situation when they began their conversation seemed to dissolve, as they allowed the unspoken feelings of the past several years to be known. He captured her heart when she first came to the village, but as a woman, she didn't know if she should be the one to voice her desire.

~ * ~

War did come. With the fighting, Hawk watched as Simon went to join the Freedom Fighters, Thomas went to see to the spiritual needs of the troops and James left to become a much-needed doctor at the front lines. Only Hawk remained at the farm.

"What are your plans, Hawk?" his father asked one evening at supper.

"I plan to fight, but in my own way. Soon I will go and join my father's people. I pray they will accept me to fight with them against the people who have mistreated us."

"What if the people refuse to have you join them?"

"I have thought about what could happen. Should something like that occur, I plan to wage my personal war. In the many years I visited my father, I learned the skills necessary to fight. I am accurate with not only a rifle but also a lance, a war club, a knife and a bow and arrow."

"You are my youngest son, and I worry about you going to war. From the stories I have heard of my family in Scotland, men younger than you have fought against the British for their independence. I am proud of your commitment to the people. I know you will do your best, no matter what manner of fighting you choose. All I ask is that you return to your mother and me when this terrible time is over."

"Your pride means more than you could ever know. Save your worry for those who know they must fight, but do not have the skills to do so carefully. I will not tell you when I am leaving. I will, one day, be gone. I plan to talk to my father's people and plead my case. I would prefer to have them with me, but if I must do this alone, I will. No matter what you hear about me, remember me as your son, but do not acknowledge it if the British come to question you. I want no repercussions for my tactics to fall on you, Ma or this farm. You are the ones who mean the most to me."

Within the week, Hawk disappeared from the farm. It didn't take him long to ride to the village of his father's people.

The first person he met was his half-brother, Soaring Eagle. At fifteen, he was an adept warrior and one of the hunters as he followed in his father's footsteps.

"Brother, what brings you to the village?" Soaring Eagle greeted him.

"The colonists who call themselves Freedom Fighters are waging war against the British. I want to fight, but I am hoping the people will fight with me."

"We heard of the war at the trading post. It has been discussed among the elders and the warriors for several days."

"That is why I am here. If the people go to war, I want to fight with them."

"Your suggestion surprises me. I would have thought you would be fighting with the whites."

Hawk smiled. "All my life I have been called The Savage. Now I plan to fight in the old ways. Our freedom and lands have been denied us by the British for too long."

"I don't know if the warriors will welcome you and your skills with open arms. As you know there is concern about you being raised in a white man's household. What does your white father have to say of your decision?"

"He worries, but he understands my desire to do things my way. My brother as well as my brothers-in-law are at the front line. Simon is fighting, Thomas is ministering to the spiritual needs of the troops and James is working in one of the field hospitals. Even though Simon is accepted as a free black man, I would not be welcomed in the same way. This is not a war that I can fight with the white men who are distrustful of me. From now on, I will be called The Savage."

"You know that is not what the elders call you. Panther Tooth has always called you He Who Stands In Two Worlds."

Hawk cringed at the hated name the chief gave him as a child. It wasn't one of respect, but one of shame for the way his father allowed Ma and Pa to raise him. It didn't matter to the old chief that Pa saved his life when his mother died giving him life with her last breath. He wished he could have known her, as he knew his father, but God and the Great Spirit made their choice, when Pa saved him from certain death before he had a chance to live.

Hawk watched as Soaring Eagle left to speak with the elders. It embarrassed him to have to depend on his younger brother speaking on his behalf. As a man, he needed to show the elders his desire to help in this war in the way of people.

Before Soaring Eagle could enter the council lodge, Hawk stopped him. "I need no one to plead my case to the elders. If they are to accept or reject me, it must be to my face."

"Are you certain? Panther Tooth has…"

"I know. He has never accepted me, even when I spent time with our father. Perhaps now is the time for younger leadership. That is not my decision to make. I merely want to fight with the people in the war that is coming to our land."

Soaring Eagle stepped aside and allowed his brother to enter the council lodge alone. Hawk could see the worry on the young man's face, but this was something he needed to do for himself if he expected acceptance.

"What are you doing here, He Who Stands In Two Worlds?" the old chief asked.

"I have come because of the war the Freedom Fighters are waging against the British."

"We were just speaking of this," Dark Moon said. "What importance is it to us?"

"It is important to everyone who lives in the land. It is the British who incite the colonists against us. It is men like Pa who want to live peacefully with us. This land is large, but if the British continue to rule from across the big sea, there will always be turmoil. I want to fight them, with or without your help. I prefer to fight beside the people of my birth, but if that is not possible, I will fight alone. What I will not do is join the Freedom Fighters. My presence beside them would bring them unwanted attention from the British. I prefer to be called The Savage and take my revenge in the old way."

"What old way do you speak of?" Panther Tooth inquired.

"From my father, I learned how to fight with the weapons of the people. I know how to attack then melt back into the dark sanctuary of the forest. I have not fought in a war, but I have been prepared to be ready for anything that might come to our land. I plan to fight for both the people of my birth and those who raised me. I have access to fine horses and bring the determination of each of my fathers to this fight."

"You have made your case, Hawk," Dark Moon said. "Leave us now to discuss that which you have proposed. We know the dark shadow that hangs over this land. War is an ugly word and one we all take seriously."

Hawk left the council lodge, secure in the knowledge Dark Moon would plead his case to the elders. Even without spoken words between them, he knew the man was his ally.

From the stories his father told him, Hawk knew Dark Moon was one of the young hunters who went with Hunting Hawk and their fathers before the massacre that took the lives of the loved ones who waited for them in the village. He knew of the anguish Hunting Hawk faced when he learned his wife was dead and his son had been taken by a white man to save his life.

"I wanted you in my life," Hunting Hawk told Hawk when he was old enough to understand. "I also knew there was no way I could care for you when I wasn't certain of where I would call home. You needed the nurturing of a loving family. I could tell that Caleb MacAfee could give it to you. I knew him long before you were born. We met by accident when he first came to our land. He came to the village and asked for permission to build his farm. The elders were impressed to think a white man would ask for their blessing on the new life he wanted to start. Over the years, he and his family befriended us often. Many of our young men, me included, helped him on his farm and learned how to care for and train the horses. In return, he made certain we had some of his horses. Since money meant nothing to the people, he compensated them in the best way he could.

"You are blessed to have two fathers who love you. Never forget not only the man who gave you life but the man who saved your life. We both love you and want only the best for you."

Why did this deeply buried conversation came to mind now Hawk didn't know. He felt this was a sign that the people would accept him and help eradicate the hated British from the land they once called their own.

"The council has made its decision," Dark Moon said, breaking into the memories of Hunting Hawk and the many things he taught Hawk.

"Do I fight this war alone or…"

"You are like your father and brother. You jump to conclusions before you know the truth. I've been sent to tell you that the warriors are ready to join you. Like the colonists, we have suffered at the hands of the men our people have heard the Freedom Fighters call the Red Coats. We first heard the name at the trading post and after seeing their soldiers, we understand why they are called by such an offensive thing."

"In that case, you know more than I do. What are you talking about?"

"They do not dress to fight in this country. Their clothing is heavy and restrictive. It might suffice in the winter but not in the summer, when the heat becomes oppressive."

Hawk contemplated Dark Moon's words. Even though the summer hadn't reached its peak, His friend was bare chested and wore a breechcloth. Many times, when he visited his father, he dressed in the same manner. He made a mental note to change his wardrobe to fit in with the people of his birth.

"Do you think there is one of the women who would help me change this clothing for something more suitable?"

"My wife, as well as the other women, would be more than happy to help you. They would also keep your white clothes for when you are not fighting. In that way, you will not bring attention to yourself."

~ * ~

Rather than staying with Soaring Eagle in the bachelor's lodge, Hawk unpacked the tent he'd used as a child when he wanted to sleep under the stars. He could see no need to build a proper lodge in the village. He also didn't want to share a lodge with the young men who looked for maidens to take to their beds.

"I cannot understand why you don't want a proper lodge," Soaring Eagle protested, when Hawk turned down his invitation to join the bachelors.

"I prefer to be alone. I am more comfortable in my tent. I can take it with me wherever I go. It gives me the solitude I need."

"Our father told me of you love of sleeping outdoors. He said it is your way, even though I never understood your need for solitude. What woman would want to sleep in such a primitive way?"

"I have no interest in entertaining a woman. She would only be a division from the path I have planned for my life. For now, I am a warrior and need to concentrate on the war that is surely coming."

Soaring Eagle shook his head and returned to the bachelor's lodge. Hawk knew his brother was more concerned with the need of a woman in his bed than what was to come.

Hawk finished setting up his tent and stripped off his shirt. The breeze that caressed his upper body invigorated him. He was, once again, a child, free of the clothing the white world dictated he wear.

"You are halfway there, my friend," Dark Moon said as he approached the camp Hawk set up for himself.

Hawk noticed the bundle of clothing his friend carried. "I didn't know your wife was so adept with a needle. How did she have time to make these."

"She didn't. These were mine. She insisted I needed new garments since I was successful in this year's hunt and provided her with the leather made from the deer I killed for the people. She assures me there is than enough left for you. I doubt you know it, but her mother and your mother were sisters. Her mother was older and came to this village as a young maiden. Your mother was the daughter of their father's second wife, as Soaring Eagle is the son of your father's second wife. That said, she considers you as family."

Hawk beamed at the new information he'd heard for the first time. It was no wonder his father came to this village, after the massacre. Here, he was still close to his dead wife's family.

~ * ~

Hawk had been in the village for two weeks, training with the warriors. As he drifted off to sleep, he realized how easy he had it at MacAfee Farm. He was past his muscles aching from physical exertion. Now he was exhausted and ready to sleep for the night. He knew once they joined the battle, sleep would be at a premium.

Tonight, the coveted sleep came quickly and was filled with dreams. In them he saw his brother-in-law fighting and his brother tending to the wounded.

"The war has begun," the James in his dream said. "It is time for you and your warriors to begin your campaign against the enemy."

Hawk awoke with a start. "Did I have a dream or a premonition?" he asked of the night sky.

Somehow, he knew this was no normal dream. James was right. It was time for the warriors to strike against the enemy.

Rousing himself from his tent, he made his way to the common area of the village, where a fire burned brightly.

"It is time," Dark Moon greeted him. "The shaman has had a vision."

"I too, had a vision. In it, my brother, James, told me it's time for us to fight."

"You have more abilities than I thought. When this war is over, you must confer with the shaman. You have a power that is usually given only to those of his line."

"When this is over, I will return to MacAfee Farm. That is where my destiny lies. I will breed and sell the best horses available in the colonies."

"We will see," Dark Moon said with a slight chuckle in his voice.

~ * ~

The Red Coats marched in perfect formation, making them an easy target for Hawk and the warriors.

Their attack was swift and without warning, not giving the Red Coats time to react to their arrival. With the fight finished, many Red Coats lay dead or dying.

Hawk made his way to one of the wounded soldiers. "Who are you?" the young man asked.

"I am The Savage. This day, your life will be saved so you can warn your superior officers to end this war."

"Why do you speak our language so well?"

"That is nothing for you to worry about. If you must know, the British have been in this area for a long time and learning their language was necessary to trade with those who see us as men and not animals."

"You are animals. Your skin is different. You don't belong among civilized people."

Hawk's blood boiled with anger. Even though he told the young man he would spare his life, the man's spiteful attitude sealed his fate.

With one fell sweep, Hawk drew his knife across the man's exposed throat. As the life blood drained from his body, Hawk turned and melted back into the darkness of the forest.

"I thought you were going to leave the soldier alive."

"That was my plan until he called us animals. They are the invaders. The man didn't deserve to live."

~ * ~

Close to where the confrontation between The Savage and his friend, Joshua, took place, one lone survivor of the attack played dead. Had he not done so, he would have suffered the same fate as his friend.

He had been conscripted into service while still in England. Back then he had no idea what he would find in the New World. What he did know was that he needed to survive and warn his superiors of the threat posed by The Savage.

Chapter Six

The war came and the fighting was fierce. The men of the MacAfee farm each went in their own direction. Simon was the first to leave. For the first time since arriving in the village, his forge was cold. As they had for years before he arrived, people turn to Caleb and his blacksmith to care for the men who were in need.

Where Simon fought was a mystery, but occasionally, Ella received word that he was still alive and fighting for the freedom everyone was hoping to obtain.

Thomas was with a unit fighting near Pennsylvania. His position as a minister kept him out of danger, so he was able to send sporadic letters to Elizabeth, praying for her safety. Since she'd taken over the duties at the church, she spent most of her time at the farm and returned to the village on Sunday to perform the weekly services of prayer and hymns.

Hawk occasionally returned to the farm from the fighting. He was like a ghost. Often Caleb heard about The Savage and the way he fought for freedom from the British. Caleb worried about all the men from MacAfee farm, but perhaps a bit more for Hawk because he was the youngest. He and Simon were the ones who were amid the fighting and in the most danger.

James was the last to leave. After receiving a message from General Washington, he joined the medical corpse who followed Washington's men, so he could attend to the wounded and dying.

Sophie, like Elizabeth, received letters from her husband, while she cared for the patients he'd left behind when he followed the men who wanted to bring forth a new nation.

~ * ~

The bell above the door to the store signaled the arrival of a customer. These days, there were only women and children who came to her establishment; therefore, Becky was anxious to see who was coming in to make purchases.

To her surprise, Uncle Richard and Aunt Mary stood just inside the door.

"What are you doing here?" she asked, after embracing them.

"Philadelphia is chaotic," Mary said. "We made the decision to leave when the Red Coats insisted on taking over our store, as well as our home. They have even taken over your old house from its new owners to billet their soldiers. There is nothing left for us. We are hoping you will be able to give us refuge."

"Of course. Stephen has gone off to fight. When he left, I insisted his wife, Beatrice, move in with me. God knows I have the room for her in my upper apartment. Their house is empty. Until this war is over it should suit your needs and give you time to make other plans."

"What of the young Indian boy?" Richard inquired.

"Hawk is fighting his own war, with his father's people. He returns to the farm occasionally. I've seen him, but he is careful not to encounter any of the British troops who might be in the area. I have heard the English have put a high price for the capture of 'The Savage'. Other than by that hated name, he is unknown to the British."

"If you are worried about your supplies, there is no need. I still have my connections. Your inventory should be arriving any day now."

Becky breathed a sigh of relief. When she first saw her aunt and uncle, she worried about not being able to cater to the needs of her customers. Many of them were women whose husbands were off fighting the war. The hardship of not being able to get supplies, coupled with running their husbands' farms and businesses, would become a breaking point for many of them.

"I heard you talking with customers, do you need some help?"

Becky turned at the sound of Beatrice's voice. "They aren't customers," she assured the woman who had been her companion for the past few years. "I want you to meet my Uncle Richard and Aunt Mary Peters. They have had their property in Philadelphia confiscated by the British and are relocating here. I told them until they can build a home of their own, they can use your house."

"Of course, they can. I'm certain everything deserves the touch of a boom and a dust cloth, but I can take care of that. For now, I have prepared supper. You know there will be enough to share. Had I known we were entertaining guests, I would have made more, but the venison roast we took in as barter will be plenty. I will open an extra jar of the vegetables we have in the pantry. By the time you close the store I should have everything on the table."

"Barter?" Richard questioned as Beatrice returned to the upper apartment.

"Money is tight. Barter is good for those who cannot afford to pay for supplies. In return I can either use them for our meals or sell them to other customers. The venison is for us. There is an older man who hunts for the women who are doing the work left by their husbands. He always brings some of his meat to the store, no questions asked, and no compensation required. I always make certain his wife gets a little extra when she comes in for supplies. It works well."

"It must, I can see by the numbers you have sent me, you are making a profit. I never thought about barter. It appears you are making it work to your advantage."

~ * ~

Hawk settled down for the night. It had been a productive day. To the British he was known as 'The Savage'. In that persona he'd carried out another successful raid on the troops everyone referred to as 'The Red Coats'.

Their regimented way of fighting gave him an advantage. He fought with stealth and the element of surprise. Even the 'Freedom Fighters' adapted his methods. He'd been successful and was proud of his achievements.

"You amaze me, Hawk," his younger half-brother said. "Night after night, you sleep alone when there are many beautiful maidens who would gladly grace your sleeping furs. A man is not meant to sleep alone every night."

Visions of Becky filled Hawk's mind. She was he only woman he wanted in his bed. To do as his brother said, would defile the promise he made to her before he left to fight the war. What he once thought would be a skirmish of a few weeks or months at the most dragged on for years.

Early in the fighting, he'd seen his friend, Dark Moon, fall to a British musket ball. He was unable to bury his friend. Instead, he, and his companions melted back into the dark recesses of the forest. It was late that night, after the British moved on, that they returned to bury their dead. In an attempt at humiliation of the dead enemy, they stripped the bodies of their clothing and weapons, leaving them naked for the predators who were already gathering to feed on the soon to be rotting flesh.

"I have no desire for a maiden. I leave them to you. For me, there is only Becky. When this war is ended, I will return home and pray she is still waiting for me."

"She's white. As a child, she could look past the differences. Do you think it will be the same today? You're a hardened fighter and have been living with your people for several years. You're not the young man who left the white world to fight for what you think is right. Remember what was done in your village on the day you were born. Just because you fought to free this land from the hold of the British does not change the color of your skin."

Hawk ordered his brother to leave him alone with his thoughts. Everything Soaring Eagle said was right. He was different from the people who raised him. In childhood, he'd been loved unconditionally, but would things be different when he returned to the home he loved?

His thoughts turned to the horses he cared for as a child and hoped to breed as an adult. They were lifeblood of MacAfee farm. On the times he was able to return home, he could tell his father was aging under the work involved in keeping the farm as well as the horses prospering.

"We need to end this war," he said to the night wind. "James' letter to father says the end is near. I pray he is correct. Life needs to return to normal."

~ * ~

A lull in the fighting gave Hawk a chance to sneak back to the MacAfee farm, the house he still called home and the people he called family. To his surprise, James was also at the farm for a long overdue reunion with his wife and children.

"Hawk, it's good to see you," James greeted him. "I've been hearing good things about 'The Savage'. George is impressed with your accomplishments. I think he would like to have you in his army, but he has no idea we are brothers."

"I can't believe General Washington even knows who I am."

"You underestimate yourself and the good you have done for the 'Freedom Fighters'. All the troops know of The Savage. They are all in awe of you. They are good at sneak attacks, but they cannot melt back into the forest and disappear as you and your warriors do."

Hawk smiled at the compliment. "They are not my warriors. I am no leader. My friend was the leader of the warriors until a British musket ball took his life. I only carry on the way he taught me. More than anything else, I want this war to end so I can return to this farm and work with the horses. Once I have reestablished myself, I will ask Becky to marry me."

"From what I hear, she waits for your return as well. You are wise to reestablish your position here and become stable before you approach her with your proposal. She has become a shrewd businesswoman and is no one you will be able to control. She certainly isn't like our mother. She may be content to move to the farm, but she will still want to oversee the running of the store daily. She is more like our sister Ella than you may think."

Hawk thought about Ella. She was indeed a strong woman. Not only did she run her restaurant, but she was also now a widow with two growing children to nurture. She was lucky to have their parents to help with the children, as they did for those of James and Sophie.

Luckily, Ella had Susan to help her with the restaurant. The two of them became good business partners and served excellent meals, sometimes without taking pay for them from the people who were unable to spend the money necessary to buy them.

He was proud of the women in his family. They were keeping the village alive, while their husbands and sons were fighting for the freedom of a new country. When the war was won, that country would emerge as the United States of America.

Hawk's mind went to the worry of what would happen should the Red Coats win the war. All hopes for a new nation would be dashed and those who fought with the Freedom Fighters could face death for the insurrection. It was bad enough many young men already lost their lives in the fighting, to lose more in the aftermath would be disastrous.

~ * ~

The relief Becky felt when her aunt and uncle arrived in the village was short lived. Although she thought Uncle Richard would be of help in the store, he felt working with the public was beneath him. He took over the bookwork but made no effort to help in any other way.

Sweet Aunt Mary showed her true colors. In Philadelphia, she'd been a member of the city's high society. Here, she made certain everyone knew she considered herself to be far superior to the people Becky served at the store daily. She also refused to cook any meals from the bartered food. Instead, she insisted she needed a cook who knew how to prepare the fresh venison and the canned vegetables. With all the women busy keeping their husbands' businesses and farms functioning, the position fell to Beatrice to fulfil. Aunt Mary also insisted Beatrice do the cleaning, as such menial tasks seemed to be beneath her. Instead, while Beatrice worked as an unpaid maid, Mary sat with her embroidery, making pieces of linen to replace the things she left behind in Philadelphia.

"What can I do to help you in the store today?" Beatrice asked as she prepared to go to the small home she and Stephen once shared.

"You do enough by working for my aunt. I can handle things here. I would prefer you to use whatever spare time you have resting. I don't understand how my aunt changed so much. I never remember her having household help."

"This has been a big adjustment for your aunt. She does have a good heart, but she is used to being a benefactor, helping the poor. Now she is no different than anyone else in and around the village. No one looks at her like she's special. She doesn't know how to be like her neighbors."

"You're more understanding that I am. My aunt used to be there for me whenever I needed her. Since they arrived here, I have hardly seen her. When she wants to communicate with me, she sends a message through you.

"In other words, I no longer have a family. My father is God only knows where. My uncle is more interested in the money the store makes for him, and my aunt has decided she's much better than I will ever be."

"You have Stephen and me. When this war is over, if this war is over, we will build a home of our own and…"

"You have a home."

"Not anymore. Your aunt has plans to make it into a grand mansion worthy of her station in life. It's as though it always belonged to the store. I have been saving the money you paid me for working in the store and looking at a parcel of vacant land here in the village. The day when Stephen comes home, we will begin building a new home, if you can put up with us while it's being built."

"As far as I'm concerned, you and Stephen could stay here forever, but I know you will want your privacy to start your family. Anything I can do to help you build your new home will give me great pleasure."

Once Beatrice left to go to fulfil her duties for Aunt Mary, Becky gave into the tears she refused to shed in front of anyone. Soon the store would be open for business and there would be no time for crying over the path her life took would be over. She had a store to run, living quarters to clean and meals to prepare, in case Beatrice was unable to do so.

She was also opened a trading post close to the Indian village where Hawk's brother Soaring Eagle lived. Earlier she opened it for the profits she could glean from it. It soon became the women and older men who visited the store for the items she could provide to them. They did so much fighting in the war it was only proper for her to see to their needs as well as those of the people who were already customers.

~ * ~

The war was winding down. It was evident to Soaring Eagle that the British were becoming less aggressive. Still there were battles to be fought.

Far from home, the men following Hawk engaged the Red Coats. Amid the fighting, Soaring Eagle saw his brother fall to a musket bullet. Leaving the others to fight, he rushed to his brother's side. It was imperative that Hawk not be captured. If he were, it would mean death for the crimes of the mythical savage. Others had fallen to similar fates, to eliminate The Savage.

"How bad is the wound?" Soaring Eagle asked.

"It is but a shoulder wound. I need to see the shaman, but I cannot continue to fight. I feel weak."

"I will take you away from the fighting. Others will continue against the Red Coats. For now, we must see to your wound before an infection sets in."

Soaring Eagle knew his words were lost on his brother, as he was no longer conscious. Getting him to the shaman whose quarters were deep in the woods was imperative.

Lifting Hawk into his arms, he carried his brother to the hidden area in the forest where the horses were tied. The young brave who tended the horses helped him to mount his horse while cradling his brother in his arms. Hawk's horse, a beautiful black, called Dark Thunder, was tethered to Soaring Eagle's horse, so as not to be lost.

Deep in the forest sat the shaman's lodge. The son of the old shaman, he'd learned how to care for the warriors who were fighting a much different war than ever before. Even so, Soaring Eagle knew the musket ball was embedded deeply in his brother's shoulder.

"I brought him to you as quickly as I could," he said, as the shaman helped him to take Hawk's unconscious body into the lodge.

"I will do my best, but it is possible he will lose the full strength in his left arm. Hawk was a strong young man, but the fighting has taken away much of his strength. The healing will take longer than it would have before this war began."

Soaring Eagle understood. From the stories told around the campfire, he knew battles never lasted as long as this fight against the Red Coats. It wasn't just the Red Coats who were tired. The warriors were ready for this to be over, but they knew they needed to fight until it ended, no matter what the outcome.

Chapter Seven

The war was over. The Freedom Fighters beat back the British and the United States of America was born.

One by one the men returned to the village. Although Simon lay buried in an unmarked grave, Stephen returned, taking much of the stress of running the store from Becky. His life had been spared, but at a cost. In the last battle he fought, he lost his left eye. Now a black patch covered the empty socket where his eye used to be.

Although the home he'd built with Beatrice was now a mansion where the owners of the store lived, he wasn't discouraged. Instead, he and Beatrice started making plans to build a new home on a plot of land not far from the store.

The last to return were James and Thomas. Their services were required long after the fighting ended. Wounded men still needed attention to continue their healing. Thomas ministered to many of the young men who fought and didn't have the spiritual leadership they needed.

Finally, they were both able to return to their home village and resume their original calling of helping the people they'd known for many years.

The only member of the society who hadn't returned was Hawk. Becky searched the pews of the church every Sunday in the hopes of seeing him sitting with his parents.

As the weeks went by, she wondered if he would ever return. Had he been killed in many of the battles? She'd heard of the hit and run exploits of 'The Savage' knowing they were talking about Hawk. He'd been daring and inflicted much military damage on the Red Coats. Had one of those battles ended in defeat?

"Have you heard from Hawk?" she asked of Caleb one Sunday after services.

"Not for several weeks. It's hard to get letters through, especially with the British trying to block all outgoing communications."

Tears welled up behind Becky's eyes, but she refused to shed them. "The British have been defeated. Others are coming home. Hawk's absence can only mean one thing. I don't want to think about it, but he could have been killed. Since he's not in the military, we might never know."

"My son isn't dead. I would know. We must be patient. He's been fighting for several years. The last time he was able to come home, I could see the toll this war has taken on him. It is possible he is taking some time to rest before he returns to us."

Becky nodded even though she had doubts about what Caleb was telling her. Hawk wasn't coming home. She would have to build on the life she'd lived since her father left her. The store was her responsibility.

~ * ~

Hawk sought the comfort of his furs in his tent on the fringes of the village. He was war weary. Absently he rubbed his left shoulder where he'd taken the musket ball during the last battle. Although it healed enough for him to return to the village, it still ached when the weather changed. Today, rain pounded on the outside of his tent further aggravating the wound.

Thankfully, the war ended weeks ago and the British surrendered. Unfortunately, they weren't back across the ocean. Instead, they fled to Canada. It was entirely possible they could strike again. The question was when. If war did erupt again, Hawk knew the days of his fighting were ended.

He also wondered about his ability to return to MacAfee Farm to breed and train the horses. They were not only the lifeblood of the farm, but also work he missed doing daily.

"One of the maidens sent you some stew," Soaring Eagle announced as he stooped to enter the tent.

Hawk marveled at how the war turned his younger brother from a teenage to a seasoned warrior. Upon returning to their village, he sought out the maiden he courted when he was an irresponsible younger version of the man who stood beside him today.

"Do I need to ask who sent this?' Hawk inquired.

"You know you don't. It came from Summer's Breeze. She has consented to being my wife and providing you with nourishment is her way of showing her favor for me."

"I am happy for you. I fear I have stayed away for much too long. It is possible Becky has found a man to share her life. God knows there are many men returning to the area and new men moving in. She is a beautiful woman, and any man would be a fool not to try to court her."

"You underestimate her. It is time for you to return to your white family. Your father needs you to run the farm and care for the horses."

"I agree with you. I pray I have rested enough. If Becky hasn't waited for me, so be it. As soon as I witness the joining of you and Summer's Breeze, I will be returning to MacAfee Farm."

"That's what I wanted to hear you say. We will be joined before the full moon rises. Already, she carries my child. It's time for you to give up your life here and embrace the one that waits for you."

Hawk wanted to spend more time with his brother, but he didn't stop him from leaving the tent. As much as Soaring Eagle wanted to spend time with Summer's Breeze, Hawk wanted some time alone to contemplate returning to the life he left behind to fight the Red Coats.

~ * ~

Although Caleb didn't want to believe his youngest son had been killed during the war, Becky did make sense. With no communication from Hawk for several weeks, he was beginning to give up hope.

He could tell Maude was also worried about Hawk. He had aways been his own person, changing his name when he was little more than a child. He came and went on his own schedule. Many times, he would disappear to go to the Indian village where his father lived.

Hunting Hawk said some of the people in the village called his son He Who Stands In Two Worlds. Caleb knew the name aptly described his youngest son. Although he'd been raised in the white world, his heart was with his father's people. It was possible he met a maiden who caught his eye, and he would be staying with the people of his birth.

A commotion in the door yard distracted Caleb from his dark thoughts. If the reason for the commotion was for a buyer looking for horses, he needed to put on a friendly front. After taking a moment to adjust his thoughts, he opened the front door. To his surprise, there was no buyer.

~ * ~

Hawk watched as Soaring Eagle and Summer's Breeze were joined. Rather than stay for the planned celebration, he went back to his tent, changed into his white clothes, and prepared to leave for MacAfee farm.

He knew he would miss the freedom of the buckskins and other trappings of his father's people. In comparison, the stiffness of the clothing of his other life seemed alien to him. He knew it would soon become as comfortable as it had been when he was growing up. It was as though he'd gained muscle, while he'd lost weight.

It was surprising how these clothes that fit so perfectly before the war were tight in some places and yet hung loosely in others.

Earlier, he said his goodbyes and promised to return when he received word of the birth of the newly joined couple's first child.

It didn't take long for him to pack his tent and the belongings he decided to take with him on the journey back to life he left behind when the war broke out. Along with the white man's clothes, he also brought along three pairs of buckskins as well as a breech cloth. He knew there would be times when he would welcome the comfort of the buckskins he'd been wearing since the beginning of the war.

In the distance, the sound of drums and singing assured Hawk, his brother's marriage, was being celebrated. He wondered if he would ever have such a celebration with Becky, or if she was now married to someone else and perhaps even carrying his child.

Refusing to think of such things, he made his way back to the home where he grew up. He knew the journey would take at least two, if not three, days depending on his strength. Whatever it took, the further he rode, the more excited he became. Soon he would be back with his parents as well as his sisters and hopefully his brother. He'd heard of Simon's death and prayed for Thomas' safety. Of course, Thomas, like James, wasn't involved in the fighting. While James saw to the physical needs of the Freedom Fighters, Thomas ministered to their spiritual needs.

To Hawk, it seemed as though the sky was a more brilliant blue, and the birds sang with a more jubilant tone than what he'd heard during the time when he was fighting,

The whole world is brighter now that we are free of the British rule. Even the birds of the air sense the change and rejoice in it.

After three days of traveling, Hawk knew that he'd ridden onto MacAfee land. Fine horses grazed in one of the far pastures. Yearlings raced across the grassy land while studs and damns perpetuated new life that would come forth in the following spring.

"I'm home," he shouted to the wind. "This is where my destiny lies. Just seeing these horses stirs my soul. The foals that are being implanted today are my future. I am anxious to return to doing what I love."

The ride from the far pasture to the main house took less than half an hour. It was close to supper time when he rode into the familiar door yard.

Dogs that had been born since the last time he was able to come home greeted him with excited barking. At the house, the front door opened, and he saw his father step out onto the porch.

Hawk urged his horse forward and dismounted before rushing to his father's side.

"Hawk, you're home."

"I'm home to stay, Pa. I've had my fill of fighting. I know where my place in this world is. I need to be here, if you will have me."

"Have you? I've prayed for your return since the day you left. From what I can see, I think it's time for some of your mother's good cooking. If I'm not mistaken, she has supper cooking."

Hawk smiled. Leaving his horse in the care of one of the grooms his father employed, he entered the familiar house. The aroma from the kitchen made his stomach ache in anticipation of eating a real and true meal.

To his surprise, the dining room table was set to accommodate three people. "You're expecting company. I don't want to intrude."

"You are the company we're expecting. Ever since the war ended, your mother set the table for three. She has never given up hope of your return to us. You are our youngest son and it's time for you to come home. I'm getting too old to work the horses in the same way as you do. You have a natural talent where they are concerned."

Hawk rubbed his shoulder. He understood he might not be able to take over as soon as his father wished him to.

"I was wounded in the last battle I fought. I may not be able to take over until the healing is complete."

"We all have wounds, both mental and physical to heal. Tomorrow I will send for James to come out and check on your shoulder. For now, I think it's time for you to go out to the kitchen and greet your mother."

~ * ~

Maude could hear voices coming from the front of the house. She wondered who would be rude enough to come to visit at supper time. It didn't matter, as she always prepared enough food to share.

She dipped hot water from the kettle she kept boiling on the stove into a waiting bowl. Once the cooking was completed, she liked to wash her hands before serving the meal. With her hands washed to her approval, she wiped them on her apron and prepared to greet whoever their visitor may be.

Turning from the sink she was shocked and pleased to see Hawk standing in the doorway. "Hawk, my baby is home."

"Yes, Ma, I'm home to stay."

Embracing him, she realized just how thin his body had become. "Are you well? You are so thin."

"I'm well now that I'm home. I'm certain your good cooking will put weight back on my body. During the journey between my brother's village and here, all I could think of was eating one of your delicious meals. I have no desire to ever eat dried meat again."

"In that case, take your place at the table. Everything is ready to be served, and I've never enjoyed serving a meal as much as I anticipate serving you on your first night home, where you belong."

"Pa told me you've set the table for me ever since the end of the war. Thank God I can return here. Pa already knows I was wounded during my last battle with the Red Coats. He is sending word to James to come out here tomorrow and check me over."

Tears pooled in Maude's eyes. Although she knew her youngest son fought the Red Coats, she now realized her worst nightmare came true. Someone had hurt the baby she'd taken into her home and raised as her own. He would heal, but at what price to his emotional wellbeing?

~ * ~

Hawk awoke in the feather bead he'd enjoyed as a child. The softness of it embraced his body and tempted him to remain there, even though he knew it was time to be up and working with the horses.

The aroma of bacon wafted to his upstairs bedroom, enticing him to get up and start the day. Once he got up, he was surprised not to feel the pain he'd become used to over the past few weeks. His shoulder was stiff, but not painful. He wondered if sleeping in his soft bed made the difference or was it because he finally came home.

After washing up and dressing for the day, he hurried downstairs to partake of the breakfast he knew his mother was preparing.

"I wondered how long you would sleep," James greeted him.

"Pa said you were coming here today. I certainly didn't expect to see you so early."

"I didn't want to miss one of Ma's breakfasts. Besides, I needed to bring out the children. They usually come out here on Saturday, so Sophie can help me in the office. Once we finish eating, I want to examine your wound."

"That's what Pa said. To my surprise, it didn't hurt as much this morning it has in the past."

"It could be that you were homesick. It's good to have you here, little brother. Now, let's get something to eat so I can do my examination and get back to my patients in the village."

Hawk eyed the breakfast table, in awe of everything his mother prepared. The bacon was accompanied with fried eggs, thick slices of homemade bread toasted to perfection and slathered in creamy butter, along with fresh strawberries floating in rich cream.

"I've dreamed of meals like these," Hawk professed once grace was said, and the food was passed from diner to diner.

"I've dreamed of having you at this table," Maude said. "I can hardly wait for tomorrow when all my children will be here for a family dinner. You have nieces and nephews who are growing up to be productive citizens as well as good students."

Last night, he'd been so happy to be home, he hadn't taken the time to assess his parents. This morning, he could see how they aged. His mother's brown hair was streaked with grey and his father's face showed worry lines. His hair wasn't as red as it had been as a young man, and his stride wasn't as brisk.

Hopefully, he would be able to take some of the burden from his father's shoulders now that he was back home.

"You aren't eating," his mother observed. "Is something wrong with the food?"

"Nothing is wrong, Ma. I'm taking a moment to enjoy being home, surrounded by family. While I was gone, I realized this is where I belong, where I want to be."

With breakfast finished, Hawk and James went up to Hawk's bedroom. After removing his shirt, he winced only slightly when James did the examination of his injured left shoulder.

"You have had good care," James observed. "It was a clean wound that was well tended. Who was the doctor who treated you?"

"It was the young shaman. He removed the musket ball and bandaged the wound."

"I'm glad your father's people have such a talented healer. I wish he was here to help me with my practice."

"If it weren't for my love of working with the horses, it is possible I could fill that position. Before the beginning of the war, the old shaman and I shared the same vision. He wanted me to train with him, but I knew it wasn't the path my life would take. Are you looking to increase your practice?"

"There are more people moving into the area. It won't be long before another doctor will be needed. I've been in contact with my brother-in-law in Philadelphia and he is visiting the medical school to see if there is someone who might be interested in joining my office."

Hawk wondered if he dared to broach the subject of Becky. He was certain James would know if the woman he loved married someone else while he delayed his return to the white world.

"What of Becky?" he finally asked.

"From what I can see, she works too hard. Thank God Stephen returned. Although he was wounded and lost his left eye, he has taken some of the burden from her. Unfortunately, since the war almost decimated Philadelphia, her aunt and uncle came here to find refuge from the British. They have been very demanding of everything from how Becky runs the store to insisting Stephen's wife, Beatrice, cook and clean for them. What help Becky had from Beatrice was taken away from her. Since I returned, I have been insisting on her getting more rest, but she feels responsible for the running of the store to say nothing of the trading . I'm afraid the only rest she gets is after church on Sunday morning. I can see her look more exhausted every week."

"Then she hasn't married anyone else."

"There have been many young men who are interested in her, but she tells them all the same thing. Her life is the store and there is no room for anyone else complicating things further."

Chapter Eight

Becky's life was in turmoil. Just last night, Stephen and Beatrice told her they were expecting a baby and Beatrice would no longer be cooking and cleaning for Uncle Richard and Aunt Mary. They were all gathered in Richard and Mary's kitchen for one of Beatrice's fabulous meals.

To say that Stephen and Beatrice's announcement was met with congratulations for the young couple was a gross understatement. The thought that Mary was going to have to find someone else to do the housework and cook was horrifying.

"What about me? What am I supposed to do without Beatrice to help me?" she whined.

"There are many new people moving into the area and I'm certain one of the young women would be more than willing to work for you."

While Aunt Mary gave Beatrice a little money from time to time, she did not consider her hired help. She came with the proceeds of the store. The cooking and cleaning were just another part of her duties. Becky knew it was wrong to take advantage of Beatrice, but unfortunately, the short-term arrangement turned into the situation they now found themselves in. If needed she would pay someone to take over Beatrice's responsibility to her aunt and uncle.

Taking one last look in the mirror, Becky decided to put last night's confrontation to the back of her mind until tomorrow. Today she needed to go to church and listen to Pastor Thomas' uplifting sermon. She needed to pray on the situation at hand and try to come up with a solution that would be agreeable to everyone involved.

With the warm weather, she didn't mind the short walk across the village square to the church. As she did each Sunday, she made her way to her usual pew, accompanied by Bernice and Stephen. Across the aisle Uncle Richard and Aunt Mary sat, staring daggers in her direction.

Instead of meeting their gaze, she bowed her head in prayer. She was certain her aunt and uncle had already been talking with the leaders of the community complaining about how she and Beatrice were letting them down.

They seemed to forget they were the ones who showed up on her doorstep asking to move into the community to leave the chaos of Philadelphia behind them. At the time, moving into Stephen and Beatrice's cottage was a temporary arrangement. It didn't take long for them to claim the home as their own and increased the size until it resembled the grand mansion they left behind in their abandonment of the city they loved.

The service began as it usually did with prayers and hymns accompanied by Susan MacAfee. She was, indeed, a talented pianist. It amazed Becky to think her friend had time to even practice with her duties at the restaurant and help Ella to care for the children.

The sermon was one of thankfulness the war was finally over and forgiveness for the Red Coats who fought only because of loyalty to their king, rather than love of the land. It ended with prayers for those who had fallen as well as the wounds of the Freedom Fighters who returned to the community.

With the final hymn finished, Becky turned to leave the sanctuary and greet Pastor Thomas. As she turned, she saw Hawk for the first time. She couldn't believe how gaunt he looked. It was as though he hadn't eaten properly in many weeks. She could only guess what his life had been like when he fought against the Red Coats.

Over the past weeks, she'd seen other soldiers return. They too looked as though the war took a terrible toll on their health.

Conditions, even under the infamous General Washington, were far from normal. Although the men didn't talk about their experiences in the presence of others they did talk to their wives. The things these women told her at the store were enough to make her sick to her stomach.

Before she could greet Hawk, Maude MacAfee came to her side. "We're having a family dinner. Would you like to join us?"

"I wouldn't want to intrude. I mean, I'm not family."

"You wouldn't be intruding. I'm certain Hawk would want you there."

"When did he get home? He looks so thin."

"I noticed that too. He arrived on Friday night. I think he would have been here sooner, but he was wounded and needed time for healing before he began the journey to bring him home."

"Wounded?"

"As he tells it, in the final battle he fought, he took a musket ball to his left shoulder. James checked him over and although he will always be weak in that arm, he is healing well. He even worked with the horses yesterday after James left."

"In that case, I would be honored to join you. Is there anything I can bring?"

"You must know the answer to that. The girls are taking over the cooking so you know there will be more than enough food for everyone. Your presence is all we desire. Susan said she would pick you up as soon as she is finished at the church. Unless there is something you must do at the store, you might want to stay here and wait for her."

~ * ~

Although his mother assured him Becky would be coming out to the farm for Sunday dinner, Hawk was still apprehensive. He thought she would seek him out after church, but she hadn't approached him.

James and the shaman both told him he would always have weakness in his left arm because of his injury. What if Becky didn't want to be married to a cripple? If that were the truth, would he be able to live his life in such proximity to her? He had no answers to his unspoken questions. He would need more time to heal and if she did accept him, she would need time to come to grips with the fact he was not the man who left to go to war so long ago.

As he stood on the porch, he saw Ella's twins approaching him. At seven years old, he knew they never knew their father. From what his mother told him; Ella learned of her pregnancy after Simon went to fight the Red Coats. He was killed before he even knew of their existence.

"Mama told us you are our Uncle Hawk. Why do you have such a strange name?" Hiram asked.

"Hawk is my middle name. I preferred it to Matthew. It suits me."

"Did you fight in the war?" Hannah inquired.

"Yes, I did. I fought with the Indians to help free us from British rule. I joined because of both my red and white families."

"Why do you have two families?" Hiram continued.

Before answering, he wondered if Ella ever explained the dynamic of the MacAfee family. "What does your mama say about our family."

His only answer was that of the vacant stare of the twins. As simply as he could, he began to explain the family into which they'd been born. "Many years ago, wonderful man by the name of Caleb MacAfee left Scotland to start a horse farm in the new world."

"That's Grandpa, right?" Hanna asked.

"Yes, that was your grandpa, my pa. He had a big heart, and he met your grandma on the ship over here. She was a widow with a young son, your uncle James. After your aunt Elizabeth was born, they thought their family was complete. It was years later that they started taking in children who were alone. I was the first, then your mama and aunt Susan."

He hoped the simple explanation would be enough to satisfy the inquisitive twins.

"Mama said you knew our papa better than anyone else in the family. What was he like?"

"Well, Hiram, I did spend a lot of time at the forge when I was younger. I wanted to learn how to shoe horses so I could better take care of the stock we grow on this farm. He was a wonderful man with a heart as big as his muscles. It took him a while to convince your mama to be his wife. He loved her more than anything in his life. As a free man, he did well with his business. I haven't had a chance to get into the village to look around, but I hear his forge is still cold."

"I hate war," Hannah said. "If we hadn't fought it, we would have known our papa."

"Many people lost loved ones, but the war was necessary. My pa says his family has been fighting the British for many generations. Freedom from England is important. Your papa gave his life for that freedom. We should thank God for the brave souls who lived and died for the love of this land."

"Why does Aunt Susan call you Baby Bird?" Hannah asked, quickly changing the subject.

The memory of Susan teasing him with her private name for him hit like a slap. "It's because I'm the youngest member of the MacAfee family. Truthfully, Susan is only two months older than me, but she liked to hold those two months over me when we were playing together,"

I'd give anything to have those days back again, but as adults, I doubt she would call me that now. Too much has happened in our lives to revert to something as silly as a childhood name.

The twins seemed to tire of the conversation with Hawk and ran off to play, just as a horse and carriage pulled into the door yard.

"It looks like the last of the clan has finally arrived," James said from behind him. "If I don't miss my guess, that is Becky sitting next to Susan. Are you sure you're up to this? It appears the trip into the village for church combined with our niece and nephew have exhausted you."

"I have to be," Hawk replied.

In truth, he was exhausted. During the trip from his father's people to MacAfee farm, it took three days of riding but did not take the energy that seemed to drain faster now that he was home. Yesterday, he worked with the horses for a little over an hour and felt his energy drain. He prayed this wouldn't be how the remainder of his life was going to be.

~ * ~

"I feel strange coming to Sunday dinner empty handed," Becky said as she climbed into Susan's carriage.

"You shouldn't feel that way. The best thing you can bring today is yourself. From what James told me yesterday; Hawk is weakened from the years of fighting and the wound he sustained. All he talks about is that he feels he has been gone for too long and someone else has stolen your heart. He needs to know you have been waiting for him. Of course, you are not the woman he left behind, just as he is not the man you remember. You have both matured far beyond your years. You need to learn who he has become. He also needs to meet the woman you are today."

Becky contemplated Susan's words. It was true, they both changed. Hawk was a shadow of himself and was war hardened. Although she'd been a successful businesswoman when the war began, she had since become responsible for her aunt and uncle as well as herself. With Stephen off fighting the war and Beatrice catering to Richard and Mary's needs, the brunt of the work in the store along with her everyday life fell on her shoulders.

"I doubt this will be the reunion I've prayed for," she finally said.

"Give it time. Start from the beginning and don't try to rush things."

Becky saw Hawk sitting on the top step leading to the porch and could not believe how exhausted he looked. Although he appeared to be gaunt when she saw him in church, he appeared to be well rested and happy to be home. Now she wondered if coming out to the farm was such a good idea. Perhaps he needed to go to bed rather than socialize for an entire afternoon.

Unfortunately, it was too late to turn back. He was already making his way toward the carriage. There was no turning back.

"Miss Becky, I'm so pleased that you were able to join us for Sunday dinner," he said as he helped her to alite from the carriage.

"What about me, Baby Bird?" Susan teased Hawk. "Aren't you going to help me? I've been so excited to see you, ever since James told me you were home."

Becky watched as Hawk walked around to the other side of the carriage to help his sister. Susan's use of the name Becky, remembered from their childhood, brought a smile to her lips. It was as though the years fell away, and they were young again.

"May I escort you to the house, Miss Becky?" Hawk asked.

"I would like that," Becky replied.

Carefully, he tucked her arm into the crook of his elbow and together they walked toward the house. Even though Becky knew she should help Susan bring in the basket of food she'd prepared earlier, she relished the attention Hawk was giving her. Thankfully, James came out to help Susan with the food. Today he was more than the town doctor, he was the older brother seeing to the needs of his siblings.

The large dining room table was set to accommodate the ten adults, while the children occupied a smaller table complete with their own serving bowls filled with food.

Everyone seemed excited to have Becky joining them. Maude made certain she sat next to Hawk. Being so close she was able to see the amount of food he put on his plate. He had only little dabs of everything the family passed to him, as though he had no appetite or desire to eat.

With dinner finally finished, Becky joined the women while the men went outside. She could only assume they went out to check on the horses, since they were the life blood of the farm.

A commotion from the front room brought attention to the women who just finished cleaning up. Becky was shocked to see James and Thomas supporting Hawk as they brought him into the house.

"What happened?" Maude questioned as she hurried to Hawk's side.

"We were looking over the horses that are ready for training, when Hawk collapsed," James replied. "He does not have the strength he thinks he should. I'm taking him up to his room so he can rest. It's going to take time for him to return to where he was when he left to fight."

As much as Becky wanted to be with Hawk, she held back. He didn't need her now, even though she needed him. Perhaps she could borrow some riding clothes and a horse to get back to the village.

"I want you to rest as well," James told Becky.

"I was thinking about that. I thought I could borrow some riding clothes and a horse to get back to the store."

What she neglected to say was that resting wasn't the only thing she planned to do at home. Being Sunday, Beatrice and Stephen would be spending the day somewhere other than the store or the mansion Richard and Mary built. There was cleaning to do both in the apartment and the store. If the MacAfee family thought, she would be resting they would never know the truth of what she did on Sunday after church.

"I'll hear nothing of that," Maude said. "There is a spare bedroom upstairs, and you will be resting. There is no need for you to ride into town. After we have supper tonight, you can go back with Susan. I agree with James, I have been worried about you for several weeks now. I even spoke with your aunt Mary about my concerns. She brushed me off saying you were stronger than anyone gave you credit for being. I didn't buy that for a minute. I have seen how she takes advantage of you and Beatrice. Tomorrow, Caleb and I will be paying Richard and Mary a visit to discuss this matter. For now, Susan will take you up to the bedroom. If necessary, she plans to stay with you until you fall asleep."

Becky felt defeated. In the past she thought she was hiding the stress of caring for her aunt and uncle while running the store. Never being one to burden others with her problems, she kept her worries buried deep within her mind.

~ * ~

Hawk damned the weakness that encompassed his body. He wanted to spend time with the horses and with Becky. Instead, James insisted he go to bed. It was embarrassing to have Thomas stay with him waiting for him to fall asleep.

"You don't need to stay with me, you know."

"I know, I also know if left to your own devices, you will be getting up and coming downstairs. I agree with James when he says you need to rest. The war was trying for many men. I should understand that as I ministered to many of them in the field hospital. They all thought the same thing, that the weakness of their bodies made them less able to care for the families they left behind. I watched them slowly regain their strength and return to their homes stronger than when they left. I'm certain you thought you were resting when you were with your father's people, but you probably did more than you should have in preparation to return home. Now is the time for the talking to end and sleep to restore your strength to come."

Hawk knew Thomas was right, but he didn't want to accept it. He closed his eyes, in the hopes that Thomas would think he was sleeping.

It didn't take long for sleep to overcome him and bring dreams of the years he spent being the dreaded Savage who persecuted the Red Coats. Each battle played out in his dreams as he watched many of his friends fall to British musket balls.

Suddenly, the dreams filled with blood and horror disappeared, to be replaced with a vision of his fathers, Hunting Hawk and Caleb.

"The time for fighting is over. Allow the healing to bring you back to the man I know you are," Hunting Hawk said. "You have made me and the ancestors proud. Caleb raised you well. He is now your one and only father."

"You know how much we all love you," Caleb continued. "Take this time for healing because there are great things to come in your future. Rest and come back to us as the young man to lead MacAfee farm in this new nation. We all have faith in your ability to run this operation when I am no longer here."

The dreams and visions dissolved, giving way to restful sleep.

Chapter Nine

"Yesterday certainly didn't turn out as we planned," Caleb said after breakfast on Monday morning.

"I couldn't believe how exhausted both of those children looked. There was no way I was going to allow Becky to borrow a horse to ride home."

Caleb chuckled at Maude's comment. "They aren't children, Maude. They are grown adults with too much responsibility on their shoulders. I did see a difference in Hawk this morning at breakfast, before he went out to check on the horses. I think the rest he took yesterday afternoon did him a world of good."

"To me they will all always be children. I did hear him tell James that he would take things easy until he regained his strength. I wish I could say the same for Becky."

"What are you talking about?"

"I'm sure you haven't noticed, but Since Richard and Mary came here, they have taken complete advantage of that girl. When the only help she had in the store was Beatrice, Mary insisted she come to cook and clean for them. Until Stephen returned from the war, Becky was running the store by herself. When they first came and William disappeared, Richard made certain she had someone to help her. It appears Becky is burning the candle at both ends.

"We need to go into the village and have a talk with Richard and Mary."

Caleb agreed and went out to get a horse hitched to the carriage. To him, Maude was a lady, the lady he loved above all others. If they were in Scotland, he would be lord of the manor, and she would be waited on hand and foot. He wondered how she would adjust to such a life. He knew the answer she would hate it. Her home and children gave her life meaning.

Thinking about Scotland brought back memories of why he came to the new world in the first place. As the younger brother, his father told him he could begin a new life breeding horses in the new world, or a member of the clergy. He'd chosen the first suggestion and never looked back. Like Maude, he loved the life he'd built for them on MacAfee farm. He was grateful to his father for allowing him to bring some good breeding stock with him.

"Did you tell Hawk where we were going?" Maude asked, as he helped her to get into the carriage.

"There was no need. He wanted to go for a ride and see the horses in the back pasture. I sent one of the grooms with him. They promised they would be back in time for dinner. I'm certain you left something out for him to eat."

"You know I did. We had several leftovers from yesterday. There is also a note on the table telling him to either help himself or go out to the cook house to eat with the grooms and stable boys."

On the way into the village, they made small talk, avoiding the reason for their trip to the village.

Finally, they arrived at the mansion Richard built for them around the small cottage that once belonged to Stephen and Beatrice.

"Caleb, to what do we owe your visit?" Richard greeted them.

"We've come to talk to you about Becky, Stephen and Beatrice."

"What about them? Becky does a good job running the store and now she has Stephen to help her. As for Beatrice, she is a bonus. I don't know what Mary would do without her."

"There is more wrong than you think. Maude and I have come to talk to you and Mary. As elders in this community, we need to speak of the situation into which you have put your niece."

"I don't understand what you're talking about. Please come into the library and enlighten us. I will get Mary and meet you there."

"Do you have any idea where the library is?" Maude asked, as they stood alone in the foyer.

"Not a clue, but we could wander around until we find it. This certainly isn't the house we helped Stephen build when he first came here. Whatever possessed Richard and Mary to take it away from the true owner of the property?"

"From what Becky has told me; they came here to get away from the chaos in Philadelphia and needed a place to live. Since Beatrice was staying with Becky, she allowed them to stay at the house until they could build one of their own. I doubt she ever expected them to take over the ownership of it."

After wandering through several rooms, Caleb and Maude finally found the library. Richad and where Mary waited for them.

"Can I get you a brandy?" Richard greeted him. "Perhaps a sherry for the ladies."

"This isn't a social call and it's far too early in the day to partake in spirits."

Richard put down the crystal decanter he'd picked up for emphasis of his invitation of enjoying a drink.

"We thought you got lost," Mary commented.

"We did," Maude said, tartly. "Since we've never been in this house since you built it to your specifications, we've never been invited."

"We were planning to have a party but with the war, it didn't seem right. We were talking about it again, but Stephen said Beatrice would no longer going to be cooking and cleaning for us."

Caleb could tell that usually mild-mannered Maude was ready to explode. This wasn't going to be pretty.

"What makes you think that Beatrice is your maid and cook? Do you pay her?"

"Pay her? Why would we. She's an employee of the store. She is paid for what work she does there. That includes…"

"It includes nothing," Maude exploded. "She cannot help at the store and refuses to take money from Becky without being able to help as she should. Added to that, she is expecting. Anyone would have to be blind not to know of her condition. I don't blame Stephen for not wanting her to overexert herself."

"Another thing," Caleb began, "is this house. Why do you think you had the right to build it into the only mansion in the village? You are not living in Philadelphia, and this house does not belong to you."

"What do you mean? The house belongs to the store."

"Perhaps you think it does because of the proximity to the store, but it belongs to Stephen. When you moved in here, it was a courtesy. Instead of looking for property to buy to build your home here, you stole the house Stephen owns. He purchased the land and with the help of the people in the area he built a small cottage that was perfect for a young married couple. Not only did you steal it. You turned it into a monstrosity that says nothing more than you are better than the people who life in and around the village."

Richard's eyes widened at the accusations Caleb made against him. As for Mary she collapsed in a chair in disbelief.

"I-I thought…"

"That's the problem, you thought rather than asked. You put Becky into a position no child should be in when her father left. Although she was a brilliant child, she was just that, a child. You should never have expected her to run and manage a store alone. True, you brought in Stephen to help her, and Beatrice helped when Stephen went to war. When you came here to escape the British, you insisted Beatrice work here all day, leaving Becky alone to run the business by herself."

"She's done a wonderful job of it, too. Even with the bartering she does, she has turned a profit every month."

"At what cost? Becky came to the farm yesterday for Sunday dinner. I saw for myself how exhausted she is. When we suggested she rest, she wanted to borrow a horse to ride back to the village. I knew if she did that, she would be catching up on the work that needed to be done both at the apartment and the store."

"I-I didn't know."

Caleb was as angry as Maude over the situation. Before this, he saw Richard as a rich businessman. He had no idea of what was going on until Maude enlightened him this morning. Beatrice wasn't un unpaid maid or cook. Stephen came back expecting to live in the cottage he'd built before the war. Instead, he realized his property had been stolen from him with no compensation to purchase more land and rebuild a home for his family that was soon to be enlarged.

Stephen and Maude deserved a place for their family, and it wasn't in the apartment above the store. If it was the last thing he did, Caleb would make certain the young couple was compensated for their loss.

~ * ~

The grandfather clock in the corner of the store chimed twelve times, signaling it was time for Becky to walk over to the restaurant for the noon meal. As usual, Ella would have a meal ready for her to take back to the store. Later in the afternoon, one of the twins would come to retrieve the dishes. She always made certain to give whichever child who came to pick up the dishes she gave them a coin for their trouble.

"I have the special ready for you, but after yesterday, I think you should sit at one of the tables to enjoy some time away from the store. Stephen is more than capable of running the things for the time you are gone."

Ella's suggestion came as a surprise. In the past, she'd never made such a request. "I shouldn't…"

"Of course you should," Ella said, leading her to the dining area where she saw Caleb and Maude sitting at one of the tables.

"Please join us," Maude said, as though this was nothing more than an unplanned meeting.

Becky sat down and waited to hear what her friends had to say about this unexpected luncheon.

"This morning, we had a meeting with Richard and Mary," Caleb began. "For some reason, Richard thought the cottage belonged to the store. Did the two of you ever talk about it?"

"I tried when he began enlarging it, but he wouldn't listen to me. Beatrice even tried to tell him the property belonged to Stephen. It was as though he turned a deaf ear to her protests. Nothing seemed to hit home until Stephen told him Beatrice would no longer work for them. I think they were horrified to think that an employee of his would have the audacity to tell him she was leaving. If you ask me, I think Aunt Mary didn't want to have to pay someone for what she felt she was entitled to having. I'd decided I'd pay someone to take over the duties Beatrice has been doing for a little bit of money here and there."

Caleb shook his head in disgust. "I made certain Richard knew he wasn't entitled to the house he's rebuilt to his satisfaction. When I left, he knew he had to pay Stephen for the home that was stolen from him. He also realizes he needs to compensate Beatrice for the work she has been doing for Mary. He thought Mary was paying the girl, but we set him straight on that point. In no way are you to spend your money to pay for the replacement help they will need to hire."

In her wildest dreams Becky never envisioned Caleb and Maude confronting Richard and Mary. To her they had been kind benefactors in Philadelphia and beyond reproach on the frontier. Even though she tried to stand up to them, they refused to listen to her. They saw her as their niece, not a shrewd businesswoman.

Tears welled in her eyes, as she blessed the MacAfee's for their help in confronting her aunt and uncle about their actions and the way they took over whatever they wanted whether it belonged to them or not. It was no wonder they were so rich in Philadelphia. If they used the same business practices as the ones here, much of what they owned was obtained underhandedly.

71

Chapter Ten

Hawk spent the morning with the grooms, learning the names and mannerisms of the horses bred for sale on MacAfee Farm. As always, he was in awe of the quality of the horses his father raised and sold for a good profit.

"I've heard many good things about you," John Ayers said. "Everyone says you are a natural with the horses. Mr. Caleb has been anxious for your return."

"I used to be," Hawk said. "With the war I've spent far too much time away. As much as I love the horses and this farm, I don't know if I'm up to the task any longer."

"I know there are many men who have returned from the war broken in spirit. That is harder to heal than the wounds you suffered. The body heals itself, at least that's what Dr. James says."

"How did you avoid being wounded?"

"I was too young to serve. When I was old enough my pa got sick, and I had to stay to support my ma and sisters. I thank Mr. Caleb every day for giving me this job. When Pa died, things got harder for our family. This job has put food on our table and clothes on our backs."

Hawk thought of the man he'd called Pa for his entire life. He had a heart that was so big and filled with love that he'd save more than young people than he could count. Had it not been for his pa, he would have died without his help and love.

"You're right, just being with these horses has sparked the desire I have to run this farm in the way Pa has run it all these years."

Even his desire couldn't keep him from heading to the house for the noon meal. Before he could get there, he remembered the note from his mother saying they would be in the village most of the day. He knew there would be food left from Sunday dinner but opted to eat with the grooms and other workers. He needed to get to know them better.

The noon meal was interesting to say the very least. All the employees were young men who were too young to fight in the war when they started working at MacAfee fram. It would be to his advantage to know these men who, one day, would be working for him.

As soon he joined the hired men, John rushed to his side. The young groom took him from person to person, introducing him as Mr. Caleb's son, Hawk.

As he greeted each young man, he saw awe in their eyes.

"What was it light to fight with the Natives?" the youngest stableboy, Willis, asked.

"In case you haven't noticed, I'm one of the natives. They are the family of my birth father, but that is a story for another day. I fought for the freedom of this land, just as your fathers and brothers did. The natives, fought to rid this country from the British. That gesture sealed their friendship. Before the massacre many of their young men worked the jobs you are doing. In payment they were given horses to breed as their own. Theirs has been a good relationship."

Immediately, the feeling in the room changed. Awe and speculation turned to acceptance and friendship. He may be older than them and hardened by the war, but he spoke to them as equals. In the future, he knew they would all work well together.

With the noon meal finished, he could feel his strength beginning to fade. Excusing himself from the company of the young men he'd gotten to know, he made his way to the house. He'd taken only a few steps when John and Willis joined him.

"We know you were wounded during the war and need time to rest," John began. "I've been watching you and want to make certain you make it to the house and your bed safely."

"Did my pa tell you to watch over me?"

"Hardly. There isn't a man in your employ who wouldn't do what we're doing. By working and eating with us, we consider you not only our employer but also our friend. Let us help you regain your strength so you can join us like the hands-on owner we have been told you were before the war called you away. Mr. Caleb is a good man but rarely comes to check on what we do daily. He loves the horses, but he's getting older and cannot always handle the work. We all respect him and would fight to the death for him, but running this farm requires young blood. You will be bringing it into the future that includes this new country."

~ * ~

Hawk considered going up to his bedroom, but he didn't have the strength to climb the stairs. Instead, he relaxed on the divan.

I'll rest for a few minutes here. It won't take long before I feel strong enough to go up and relax in my bed for a few minutes.

He took off his boots before he put his feet on the cushions of the divan. Even with his mother not in the house, he knew she wouldn't approve of anyone putting booted feet on the furniture.

To rest, he closed his eyes. Within a matter of minutes, he slipped off to sleep. It wasn't a restful sleep but one filled with dreams.

You are in the place where you belong, the Hunting Hawk in his dream said. *During the war, you did what needed to be done with the people you were meant to be with. Now, you need to be with your white father. He has trained you well. I know how good you are with the horses. Caleb needs you He is no longer a young man. Time is passing quickly for him and for you.*

Hunting Hawk is right, Son. Your mother and I love you as much as if we were your true parents, Caleb said, replacing Hunting Hawk in the dream. *Listen to his wisdom. Without him in the village, no matter how you fought beside them, you are still seen as an outsider. Allow your brother, Soaring Eagle, carry on your true father's legacy. Your future is on this farm carrying on the legacy I started so many years ago.*

The dream faded, allowing Hawk to slip into a deep and restful sleep.

~ * ~

"That was the hardest conversation I've ever had with anyone, other than my father," Caleb said as they drove the carriage toward the farm.

"I agree, but what do you mean about the conversation you had with your father? You rarely speak of your life before we met on the ship."

Caleb wished he'd never mentioned his father. The memory was a painful one. Before he began, he cleared his throat, as well as his mind.

"Back in Scotland, I have two brothers and a sister. My father raised the best horses in Scotland and sold them to buyers from all over the world. He was so successful that he purchased a second property, as well as the ship that brought us here.

"My oldest brother, Sean, moved to the second farm when he got married and continued the family business. When my next brother married, our father decided it was time to turn the main farm over to Eric.

"I worked for Eric and was twice the horseman he would ever be. He thought he was entitled to his position. Since he had Father's wisdom and my labor, he spent much of his time in the pub with his friends. Even his wife resented him.

"When I turned twenty-one, I told Father I thought I deserved to have the farm more than Eric. Instead of agreeing with me, he slapped my face and told me to leave. He even suggested I continue to work for Eric, establish myself in the new world or become a minister. Only the second options was to my liking.

"It was Sean who helped me acquire the horses I brought with me to the new world. He also used his connections to help me purchase this land. He commissioned the house and outbuildings to be erected. In return, I worked for him for the three years it took to begin what we have here today.

"Over the years, I have only had communication with Sean. Had it not been for him, I would never have known of our father's passing."

"What happened to Eric and your sister?"

"Somehow, Eric was able to hire competent help and run the farm. Unfortunately, he was not as successfully as Father. He continued to drink, and finally left everything to his oldest son, Michael, before he took his own life. According to Sean, Michael is as lazy as his father was. He lost the farm and came to Sean looking for work. Sean sent him on his way with five hundred British pounds.

"Bernadine married well but died in childbirth. Her child, a daughter, lived and her father made certain she married a wealthy man with a title. Sean says she is as much of a beauty as her mother was."

"It's no wonder you never mention them. Sean was a godsend because had he not set you up with his farm and the fine bloodlines of the horses, I would never have met you. I'm sorry I will not meet him."

"I've been thinking about that. Once Hawk has returned to health, I plan to return to Scotland and meet with Sean. Before the war began,

Sean and I were planning this reunion. I know I can't go home, since someone else owns the farm where I grew up, but I can see my family and introduce them to the beautiful woman I have called my wife all these years."

"I don't know what to say. I didn't know of the life you lived before you came here. It's a wonder you have such a big heart. Not only did you raise our son and daughter, but you took on Hawk, Ella and Susan as your own."

"They are all my own. Elizebeth is the child of my loins, but all of them are children of my heart. We've been blessed to be able to guide them in the direction their lives were meant to take. The two of us have done God's will and now it is time for us. They are the future of this village."

~ * ~

Hawk awoke to the sound of his parents entering the house. In the twilight of his sleep another dream came to him. In this dream, he saw the future. Soaring Eagle held the position their father filled for so many years as the leader of the hunters. He was also a trusted confidant to the young chief and well respected among the people.

In the same manner, he saw his future. In it he was the prosperous manager of MacAfee farm. With his siblings, he owned the property and continued to breed prime horses that were prized by wealthy landowners throughout the states of the growing nation.

"Did you get some rest?" his father asked.

"I experienced some dreams. The first was of the present and the second the future. I think we need to talk about them."

"I don't understand."

"Before the war came to our area, I was in the village of the people. In the dream, I knew it was time to fight. When I told the shaman about it, he said I had the abilities of a shaman. We would talk after the war. Unfortunately, he died while I was fighting and when I returned, I was too weak to confer with his son. I think I can see the future through dreams and visions."

"Long before you were born, Hunting Hawk and I were friends. He was always a visionary. As I recall, he predicted he would have a son who was destined for great things. Even as a young man, you fought for the freedom of this nation. I am certain he is always with you and is as proud as I am of your accomplishments. I pray I have added to your future as I know Hunting Hawk has."

Tears threatened to fall as Hawk knew he received the best traits of both of his fathers. "I promise I will continue to make you proud of me."

Chapter Eleven

ecky was concerned when her aunt and uncle requested a meeting with Stephen and Beatrice as well as her.

She heard about the confrontation between Caleb and Uncle Richard. She knew harsh words had been spoken and prayed her uncle wouldn't take out his anger on the three of them. There was no way she could run the store without help. What if Uncle Richard insisted Stephen and Beatrice leave the village so he and Aunt Mary could continue to live in the grand house?

"I'm certain you are wondering why I called this meeting," Richard began. "It has come to my attention that I have stolen the house where we are living. I honestly thought the cottage belonged to the store and when Mary wanted it to duplicate the home we left in Philadelphia, I couldn't say no,

"Caleb told me the land was purchased and the house built by Stephen. I've never been ashamed in such a way in my entire life. Mary and I have been talking about it and decided to return to Philadelphia. The house, with all the renovations will belong to Stephen."

"We couldn't," Stephen protested. "It is far too grand for us, especially with the baby on the way. We prefer a more modest home."

"We thought of that possibility as well," Mary said, speaking for the first time. "I was aware my taste is far different from yours. We would like for you to find a piece of property that suits your needs, and we will purchase it for you. We will also have a new home built for you to your specifications."

"What will become of the mansion?" Stephen inquired.

"We thought of that as well. With the war, there are many widows with children who are unable to manage the work required to run the farms left behind by their husbands. The mansion would give them a fresh start in the village and a chance of meeting someone who could become special to them. They could also find work that is more suitable for them than plowing fields and milking cows."

"What about the land they own?" Becky asked.

"There are many men returning with nowhere to go. We plan to help them buy the farms or purchase the land outright so the women who would be living at the mansion would be compensated and given the resources to start a new life."

Stephen held out his hand. "We have been looking at a piece a property not far from the store. I was going to put in an offer on it after church on Sunday. My duties will keep me busy throughout the week."

"I will go with you on Sunday," Richard said. "In the meantime, I'm certain you will be able to decide what you want your new home to be. Don't forget to make enough room for the baby who will be here soon to say nothing of those to come."

~ * ~

"That wasn't what I was expecting," Becky said once her aunt and uncle left the store. "I thought for sure they were going to take over, I certainly wouldn't put it past them."

"They certainly were generous," Stephen commented. "It's as though they knew we wouldn't be comfortable in that big house. The thought of bringing in widows with children was the perfect solution. Who do you think they have I mind managing the house?"

"It wouldn't surprise me if it was Abigaile Johns. She's older and never had children. Recently, she has been helping to care for children while their mothers work in the fields. As far as I'm concerned, she would do good job of managing the home. As for the farm she owns, she's let the land lay fallow ever since her husband died. With never having children, I'm certain she had money set aside for her old age."

Becky knew she would miss having someone to share the upstairs apartment, but she was excited to think Stephen and Beatrice would have the privacy needed to start and raise their family. Even more exciting came when the young couple asked her to help them come up with plans for the new home that was being built for them.

~ * ~

The village swarmed with activity. Stephen and Beatrice's home was being built, and many widows were anxious to sell their farms and move into the community. As Becky predicted, Abagil was thrilled to be asked to manage the home for the widows.

New farmers were moving into the area. Owning and operating their farms were erasing the horrors they'd experienced during the war.

Even Becky was making a profit by selling supplies to the new residents.

The only thing missing was Hawk. Although she saw him on Sunday in church, it was evident his recovery was taking longer than anyone expected. He'd been home for almost a year and had yet to approach her about the future.

In the meantime, many young men approached her. Her excuse was how busy she was with the store and that she wasn't interested in being courted.

~ * ~

Every day Hawk could feel his strength returning. Between his mother's good cooking and the rest, he was getting he knew it was time to talk to Becky about the future he wanted to give her.

Rather than ride his horse into the village for the church service, he took one of the carriages. He'd been home for almost a year and for the first time, he knew he was strong enough to confront Becky.

All through church, Hawk focused his attention on Becky. Rather than listening to the sermon Thomas was giving, he let his mind wander. As an adult, he realized he was no longer the young man everyone knew as Hawk. He was ready to take on his adult life and be known by his Christian name, Matthew.

With the service ending, he mustered all his courage and approached Becky. "Good morning, Becky," he said once they stood close to each other. "Would you do me the honor of taking a carriage ride and partaking of a picnic?"

He didn't realize he'd been holding his breath until she turned and smiled at him.

"I didn't think you'd ever ask. I'd be delighted to go with you. Is there any place special you had in mind for this picnic?"

"There's a lovely grove of trees and a small creek on our property. It's a very peaceful place. With the length of the war, we need to get to know each other again. I know I've grown and from what I've heard you have as well."

"You're right, we have changed. Even before the war I took on the responsibilities that should have belonged to my father. They became more demanding when the war took away many of the young men from the area, including my helper at the store. I've learned to do business in a much different way than my uncle did business in Philadelphia."

Hawk knew they would have much to talk about, including the white name he hadn't used in many years.

~ * ~

Becky walked the short distance from the church to the store so she could change to something better suited for a picnic. Just recently, she'd learned that one of the widows living in the mansion was an expert seamstress who was planning to open a dressmaker and tailor shop in the village.

Becky ordered several day dresses to be made for the store as well as some for herself. After changing into her new dress, she appraised her appearance in the full-length mirror she insisted on her father bring with them from Philadelphia. For this picnic, she wanted to look her best.

She just came downstairs when Hawk parked his carriage in front of the store. She smiled to see he, too, changed his clothes. With three siblings in the village, he could have used any of homes to make the change.

Instead of the frock coat and tricorn hat he'd worn to church, he was now clad in a white shirt and buckskin pants. From the fringe and beading on the legs of the pants, it was evident they were made by one of the Indian women from the village of his birth people.

"You look beautiful," he greeted her.

"I was going to comment on how handsome you are when you aren't dressed as formally as you were in church."

A smile crossed his lips, bringing a sparkle to his eyes she hadn't seen before.

"Yesterday is over and so is the war. I have made some decisions, and I want you to be the first to know them. For now, allow me to help you into the carriage."

Becky held out her hand as she stepped up to get into the carriage.

The weather was perfect for a picnic, and the scenery was magnificent. Even with perfection around her, she wondered what he wanted to tell her that it had to wait until they were settled in what she now considered the picnic grove.

As he told her, the grove was beautiful with birds flitting between the trees and bees buzzed amid the summer blooms of wildflowers. She watched as he spread out a blanket along with a bounteous picnic lunch.

"Which one of your sisters packed this lunch for us?" she asked once he seated himself next to her.

"I'll have you know I packed it myself. True, I did get some food from the restaurant, but I made packed the basket."

Becky laughed, trying hard to imagine Hawk bustling around the kitchen of the restaurant to find everything he needed to pack a lunch.

"When I was fighting the way, I often had to cook for the camp. I'm very good at cooking over an open campfire. Of course that is not what I wanted to tell you. In the spring, my parents will be sailing to Scotland for a long overdue reunion with my father's family. At that time, I will be taking over MacAfee Farm. In that position, it is not proper for me to be called Hawk. From this day forward I will be called Matthew or Matt. It is my given name, after all. I took the name Hawk as a rebellious child. I am now an adult with responsibilities befitting an adult."

"You will always be my Hawk, but I do understand your decision."

"Your Hawk? You…"

"I never stopped waiting for or loving you. Somehow, I knew we were destined to be together when we first met. We both had to grow and mature in our own way. We will have to decide how to live the rest of our lives. I have the store to consider saying nothing of the trading post I opened near where your birth people live, and you have the farm. There is no need for us to rush into anything."

"Are you asking me to marry you?"

"I'm saying if and when you should ask me, my answer would be yes."

"You're right, we have many things to arrange. I was going to ask you to marry me, just not this way. I still need to grow into my new position in this country."

"I understand. I have decisions to make as well. We have time to plan for our future. I am so glad you want me in your life. I'm willing to wait however long it takes."

Matt took her hand in his and brought it to his lips, to kiss it tenderly. In all the years they'd known each other the only time he'd made such a gesture was before he went away to fight the war for the freedom of the new United States.

That small gesture made her want more of his kisses and tender hugs. She wanted the kind of love his parents shared for so many years. She knew it would take time for that love to grow as they got to know the people they were today. Before this they knew each other as children, but those carefree days were over. They each had responsibilities of adulthood, and they would have to learn how to deal with them. Somehow, they would have to learn how to work together both on the farm and in the stores.

Chapter Twelve

William Hillson sat by his campfire wondering how his life had come to this. In Philadelphia he was a respected businessman. He married into a family who gave him the position of store manager at one of the largest mercantile stores in the city.

Everything went to hell in a handbasket when his wife, Amy, got sick and died, leaving him with a headstrong daughter he had no idea how to handle. To add insult to injury, his former brother-in-law insisted, they should move to the frontier and start a store in a small settlement.

The first person he met when he arrived at the settlement was Caleb MacAfee, a Scotsman who claimed two black girls and an Indian boy as his children. Who in the right mind treated people who were worthy of being nothing less than servants or slaves along with a savage as their family?

Even though one of the black girls and the savage were the same age as his daughter Becky, he insisted she have nothing to do with them.

He was further insulted when the grand house he thought would be waiting for him turned out to be little more than an apartment above the store. He couldn't believe these backwoods people would expect him to go from living in his Philadelphia mansion to the cramped quarters, without so much as help to clean and cook for him.

His resolve disappeared when Ella MacAfee came to help them get settled and teach Becky how to cook. He needed her until Becky was able to prepare a decent meal for him.

He soon heard rumors that Ella had been a bed slave when MacAfee bought her and her daughter, Susan, and gave them their freedom. It was evident Susan MacAfee was of mixed breed. There was no doubt, she was fathered by the white man who bought Ella as a bed slave. Something like that would not have been allowed in Philadelphia. Descent white people didn't socialize with people of color. MacAfee was an ignorant fool for taking them into their home.

While she was coming to teach Becky how to cook, he acted on the impulses he'd held in check since his wife died. God knew he had needs and since Ella wasn't a virgin, what harm would there be in taking her to his bed. When he advanced on her, she had the nerve to slap his face and run from the store to return to MacAfee farm.

It wasn't long before Richard Peters came to the store with a settlement of money and a horse he'd purchased from that fool Caleb MacAfee. After leaving the settlement, at his brother-in-law's request, he made his way back north. It didn't take long for William to make it to Boston, where he was able to get a position working for a general merchandise store.

When the war broke out, he decided to align himself with the British. With their highly trained forces they were sure to finish off the Freedom Fighters within a few weeks, if not months. It would serve the people who fought against them right to be arrested and executed for their crimes against the king.

The defeat of the British came as a brutal blow to William. As a Loyalist, he knew he wouldn't be welcome in Boston. His only option was to head for the frontier. There no one would know of his political affiliations.

He was now camped but a few miles from the settlement, where Becky ran the store that should have been his to manage. Living in such proximity to the settlement, now turned village, where his daughter lived, he changed his name to Robert Harris. As a drifter, he worked doing odd jobs for some of the wealthier farmers in the frontier and planning his revenge on the daughter who took everything he worked so hard to accomplish.

Thoughts of teaching his old maid daughter a lesson, he considered getting her alone and raping her, but that went against everything he'd been taught. Perhaps he could take the savings he carried with him and hire someone to do the deed for him. That would be for the best. He would find someone desperate for money and pay them to bring her to his camp so he could watch her humiliation. He heard there was an Indian village not far away. It was possible he could find one of the young bucks to do his bidding.

~ * ~

Soaring Eagle rode into the forest in search of game to feed his family. Six months earlier, his son Hunter had been born and bringing nourishing food to his lodge was imperative,

In the distance, he saw a white man bumbling his way through the thick woods. The closer the man came; it was evident he was lost and in desperate need of food.

"Do you need help?" he called out as he approached.

"You speak English?"

The man's question caught him off guard. It was well known that his people were all knowledgeable of the white man's language, as they had been dealing with the white men for many years.

"All our people speak your language. Are you lost?"

"I'm told there is an Indian village close, but I've been unable to find it."

"Who are you and why is it you seek out my people?"

There was a long pause before the man answered. "My name is Robert Harris. I'm looking to get some trade items for my store."

Soaring Eagle knew immediately the man was lying. The trading post not far from the village had been established by Hawk's woman. The man she hired to manage it was called Peter Manson and was well known to everyone in the village. Not only did he accept them, but everyone was treated fairly with their trades.

Without letting on that he didn't believe the man, he decided to take him to the village and learn his reason to seek out his people.

As a trader, Soaring Eagle thought the man would have a horse, but there was none to be seen. "Do you have a horse?"

"She is at my camp. She's getting old and riding for any distance isn't good for her. I need to get the trade goods to purchase another one."

He plans to steal one of our horses, but I think he has another reason to come to the village. Only time will tell what he wants from us. It isn't trade goods. I have caught him in a lie. How many more of them will he tell the people to get what he wants?

~ * ~

The village bustled with activity when Soaring Eagle returned. Luckily, he'd snared two rabbits for the cooking pot before he met up with the white man who called himself Robert Harris.

"You are welcome at our campfire," Spotted Eagle suggested, knowing the man needed something to eat.

"I'd rather be taken to your chief. I'm certain he can help me get what I need."

Soaring Eagle hid the smile that threatened to cross his lips. Little did this man know how close he was to Chief Running Deer.

"My woman will make certain you are comfortable and fed while I go to see Chief Running Deer. He will want you to be presented to him by the person who found him."

The trader accepted Soaring Eagle's explanation giving him the chance to confer with Running Deer.

"What brings you to my lodge?" Running Deer inquired. "Is there trouble in the village that I do not know about?"

"You might say that. While I was out hunting and checking my snares, I found a white man wandering in the forest. He says he is a trader, but I could tell he was lying to me. He insists on seeing you. I told him I needed to present him properly to you."

"I will meet with him and see if I can find out what his reason for seeking us out is. What are you thinking?"

"He is an older man, possibly the same age as what my father would have been. I can't tell you why, but I have a bad feeling about this man."

"Like your father and brother, you have the instincts of a shaman. I doubt you know, but your father decided to take a different path than his father. He was named Hunting Hawk because of a vision given to your grandfather, who was the shaman in their village. He lost his life during the massacre and your father refused to acknowledge his heritage. If you have a bad feeling about this man, I trust your instincts. When he has taken nourishment and sent to the bachelor's lodge to rest. I need to see what the young men think of him and if they share your concerns. I will meet with him tomorrow."

Soaring Eagle took his leave, thinking of what Running Deer told him. All his life he'd had prophetic dreams as he knew his brother, Hawk, did, but never thought of them as visions. For the first time, his life made sense. He would never be a shaman, but he would pay closer attention to the visions he once called dreams.

~ * ~

The man who called himself Soaring Eagle disappointed Robert. Instead of taking him to see the chief, he was left with the man's woman and a crying baby. This certainly wasn't the reception he expected. Of course, he hadn't expected these savages to speak English.

The woman brought him a bowl of stew. If he hadn't been so hungry, he wouldn't have accepted it, but it did smell good. After the first taste, he found it very good. The woman did know how to cook, even if it wasn't the beef he craved.

"I see my wife has fed you well. Chief Running Deer says he will meet with you tomorrow. For tonight, you will stay in the bachelor's lodge."

Internally, Robert was clapping his hands in glee. Externally, he pretended to be disappointed at not meeting with Running Deer. "I thought I'd see the chief today, but if I have to wait so be it."

Just thinking of the bachelor's lodge suggested most of them would be young and more than willing to do his bidding.

He allowed Soaring Eagle to escort him to the bachelor's lodge. Once there he was shown to a bed of furs. One by one, the young men began to return to the lodge from whatever duties they were responsible for.

Once they were served the evening meal by one of the women of the tribe, he proposed his idea.

"I would like you to bring me a woman."

"Aren't you too old for a woman," Spotted Pony teased.

"Not for me, but for one of you. There is an old maid in the white man's village. She can't seem to find a husband. Maybe it's because she doesn't know how to please a man. You could teach her how to be a woman and please a man."

The young men murmured among themselves. It was evident they were considering his proposition. Hopefully, within the week, he would be watching Becky be raped and degraded. In no way would anyone accept her in the village leaving the only thing she was good for was being an old whore.

~ * ~

Soaring Eagle wasn't surprised when Running Deer summoned him early the next morning.

"Several of the young braves have been to see me." Running Deer began. "You were right, the white man you brought to the village is not what he says. He wants a white woman kidnapped and raped."

"I had a vision last night," Soaring Eagle said. "In it, I saw him gloating over Becky, Hawk's woman, being kidnapped and raped. I don't know who he is, but his name is not Robert. He means only harm to her."

"I thought of Hawk's woman as well. I sent one of the young braves to MacAfee farm to get Hawk. He will be able to tell us if he knows this man."

~ * ~

Matt finished his breakfast and prepared to start his day. He knew his father was already at the stable with one of the mares that was in the throes of labor as she gave birth. They both spent the night at the stable and were taking turns eating breakfast, so someone was with her throughout the birthing process.

"There's a young man here to see you, Matt," John said as soon as Matt stepped out of the house.

"This isn't the time. I need to see to the mare and relieve my father."

"This is a young man from the Indian village, and he says it's urgent."

"We have a new stallion," his father interrupted. "Both the mare and the foal are healthy, and it was an easy birth."

Matt breathed a sigh of relief. Being the first time for the mare to give birth, he worried about having to help her bring her foal into the world.

With the concern for the next generation of MacAfee horses coming safely in the world, Matt turned his attention to the young man who waited for him. He immediately recognized Spotted Pony standing beside a horse that had been ridden hard.

"Is something wrong in the village?" he inquired.

"Yes, there is something terribly wrong. A white man came to the village and wanted one of us to kidnap and rape a white woman. It didn't take long for us to understand the woman he wants is your woman."

"Becky? Who would want to harm her?"

As soon as he voiced the question, he knew the answer. It had to be her father. For some reason he'd returned to the area and Matt knew it was for revenge against her and the business she worked so hard to build.

"Becky is in danger," he told his father. "I'm going to the Indian village and see what's going on. Spotted Pony's horse is exhausted. Will you see to him? I'll be giving him one of our stallions to increase the people's herd."

"I'm going with you. From what I heard of your conversation, 1 have a feeling I know who this man is. He is dangerous to you and Becky. I knew the man was evil the first time I met him. My opinion never changed. If it is Becky's father, I will be able to easily recognize him."

"Running Deer will make certain I am safe. Still, I would like to have you at my side. Are you certain you don't need to rest?"

"I slept off and on throughout the night, as I know you did as well. For now, we need to see if our suspicions are correct and decide how to deal with the threat to Becky."

Within the hour, Spotted Pony had eaten a meal and was ready to ride the new stallion back to the village of his people.

Matt would have left immediately, but he knew the young man who came to warn him about the man who wanted to harm Becky needed to have something to eat before they began their return to the village.

He also worried about his father. Although Spotted Pony could ride for hours without resting, he knew his father was not up to such hard riding. To be truthful, he wasn't strong enough to ride to the village without stopping to rest.

While age was his father's problem, his was the wound he suffered in the war that took the strength he needed for such a long ride. In no way could he match Spotted Pony's strength and agility. Even though he was gaining more strength every day, he knew he would never be as strong as he was before the beginning of the war.

The sun was high in the sky when they finally finished the noon meal and began the journey that would take them back to the Indian village.

Matt knew Spotted Pony was ready to begin another frenzied ride on his new stallion but was content to pace himself to accommodate Matt and his father, giving them time to rest.

They rode until late in the evening, when they finally arrived at the trading post where Matt knew they would be welcome to spend the night. In no way could his father withstand spending the night sleeping outside in the surrounding forest.

Once Caleb was settled in the extra bedroom of the trading post, Matt and Spotted Pony made camp outside. Although Matt wished he had his tent, he knew he didn't want to take the time to set it up when he was so anxious to get to the village and face the man who meant harm to Becky.

Early the next morning, Spotted Pony went hunting and returned with two squirrels to roast for their morning meal. He knew it wasn't the food his father was used to eating in the morning, but it was nourishing.

They brought the roasted meat into the trading post, where his father was ready to start the day.

"This meat reminds me of some of the meals I shared with your birth people before the massacre," Caleb said. "It was during those meals that I learned to appreciate the bounty this land has to offer. Even your mother learned to enjoy the meals she shared with the women when your sister, Elizabeth, was born. The People were very generous, coming to care for your mother after she gave birth. It was a hard time for her and being so sick, she couldn't nurse your sister as she wanted to do. The women brought out a someone who recently gave birth and was able to share her milk between the two babies."

Hearing this story for the first time brought back memories of the reason Ella and Susan were part of their family. Had it not been for Ella, he would not have survived. It was through her mother's milk that he, like Susan, thrived and grew to adulthood.

He was able to see his life in a completely different light. Women, be they be white, black, or bronze skinned, were to be cherished as givers of life. Men were the strong ones of any union, but instead it was the women who gave and nourished life, making them much stronger than any man he knew.

With the morning meal finished, they left for the last leg of their journey to the village. It was strange to think just a year ago this same trip took him three days. At the time he thought he was strong enough to return to the farm and resume the life he left behind when he went to fight in the war. Now he knew he'd only deluded himself about his physical strength. Even after a year of healing, he knew his life would never be the same again.

By early afternoon they arrived in the village. As he had been after the war, he was met with the enthusiasm of seeing a hero return to the village.

Soaring Eagle and Running Deer were the first to welcome them to the village. "We have prepared a lodge in anticipation of your arrival," Soaring Eagle said. "Although we did not expect to see Caleb come with you, there is enough room for both of you in the lodge."

"What about the man who wants to do harm to Becky?" Matt inquired.

"You are not to concern yourself about him today. He is being well guarded. You and your father have had a long journey. It is best if you rest and allow us to care for you."

Matt silently applauded his brother for taking on the responsibility of seeing to the welfare of himself and his white father.

He knew this was the first time his father visited this village. The men and women he knew from the old village were now gone and yet this younger generation embraced him as an honored guest. The rest Soaring Eagle offered was done with respect, making Matt proud of the people of his birth.

Chapter Thirteen

Anger became Robert's only companion. Instead of accepting his proposal to kidnap and rape Becky, Chief Running Deer had him physically removed from the bachelor's lodge. Now his lodging was a secluded building with only one entrance which was guarded twenty-four hours a day.

He would have thought those young men would have jumped at the chance to deflower a white woman. He certainly didn't expect for these savages to make him their prisoner. He'd seen nothing of Soaring Eagle or Spotted Pony. He thought they were men he could trust, but he was mistaken.

"Where are Soaring Eagle and Spotted Pony?" he shouted.

His question met only with silence.

Other than his guards the only person he saw was the women who brought his meals. As much as he wanted to pull one of them into the building and have his way with her, they never came alone. They were accompanied by one of the men and as soon as they delivered his meal, they left quickly.

He'd been in isolation for several days when Soaring Eagle finally appeared.

"You're to come with me."

Before Robert could leave the lodge, Soaring Eagle tied his hands with strips of leather. To add insult to injury, the man also attached a leather band around his neck and led him outside as though he was a prize horse.

"What does this mean? Why have I been treated in this manner?"

"Because you are an evil man."

Robert turned to face Caleb MacAfee for the first time in many years.

"You chose the wrong village, William. Your daughter, Becky, will be marrying my son, Matt, soon. These people hold him in high regard because of the way he fought in the war. They are the people of his birth and will protect him and his soon to be wife with their lives."

"I forbid it. Becky is my daughter. I will not see her married to a savage."

As though the word savage and the sight of Matt MacAfee triggered something in his mind his anger flared even brighter within him. "It was you," he spat. "You were The Savage. It's too bad someone didn't kill you or better yet capture you for the ransom they had on your head. I would have enjoyed seeing you locked up and executed by the British."

"No one knows who The Savage was. He no longer exists. The British have been defeated, and he is no longer needed except to help build this new country."

"If I were free, I would show Becky just how wrong what she is planning is for her future."

"You may have fathered Becky, but she is a woman who can make her own choices. She will not be a pawn in your evil plans. I know what you wanted to do to my sister, Ella. You should have been run out of the settlement at that time, but we didn't want to sully Ella's name. Thank goodness for Richard doing it for us."

"That son of a bitch betrayed me too. The last I heard, he left Philadelphia with his tail between his legs."

"He left when the British commandeered his business and his house." Caleb said. "He came to the village and when the war was over, he returned to Philadelphia to rebuild his life."

The fight seemed to go out of William. "What are you going to do with me?"

"That's not up to me," Caleb said. "You have shamed Running Deer's people with your obscene proposal. You have also put my son and soon to be daughter-in-law in danger. Justice is up to them."

"Among our people such an evil man should be put to death. What do you say, Hawk?"

"I agree. He has never been a father to Becky. When her mother died, she was little more than his bookkeeper because of her knowledge of mathematics. Once they came here, he turned her into a storekeeper, bookkeeper and unpaid maid. There is no love lost between the two of them. I agree with Running Deer. This evil must cease to exist."

"You can't kill me. I want to see my daughter. She will plead my case."

"If you want to prolong your imprisonment, I will send someone to the village to bring her here."

"Would you send a savage?"

"My father needs to return to the farm. He will check on things there and fetch her. It is possible she will not want to see you, but that is up to her."

"She'll see me. We're blood. No matter what has happened in the past, she will be happy to be reunited with her father."

"If she does come it will be at your request. It will not be out of love for you but to see you one last time before you are out of her life forever."

~ * ~

Becky was surprised when Matt and Caleb weren't in church on Sunday morning. As soon as the service ended, Becky sought out Maude.

"Where are Matt and Caleb?"

Maude paused for a moment, as though thinking of the proper answer. "Several days ago, one of the young braves came from the Indian village and said there was a white man there who was making threats against you."

"That could only be my father. I need to go out to the village. Can I stop at the farm and get a pair of Matt's buckskins?"

"You shouldn't go alone," Maude protested.

"I've driven out to the trading post in the carriage before. I know the way and can spend the night there. It will be quicker if I ride the horse."

"Come out with me. If you are set on this, you can take one of our horses. They are better adapted to being ridden than the one you use with your carriage."

Although she knew Maude's suggestion would include having Sunday dinner before she left it did make sense. She needed the time to plan for what she would do and say once she faced her father.

They arrived at the farm, just as Caleb rode into the door yard. Becky searched for the horizon to see if Matt followed him but was disappointed to see Caleb riding alone.

"Your father is a prisoner in Running Deer's village."

"I thought as much when Maude told me where you and Matt were. I want to go out there."

"That's why I'm here. Running Deer sentenced him to death for his evil plans. I am to bring you back with me so he can see you one last time before he dies."

"Death?"

"Not only his plans for you were evil but he brought shame on the people thinking they would do his bidding. Such things aren't tolerated within the village."

"When can we leave?"

"I need to rest, as does my horse. Tomorrow morning will be early enough. William is going nowhere. He is being heavily guarded. Does Stephen know of your plans?"

"Before we left church, I told him I was going out to the trading post. The less he knows of the situation, the better. He can run the store and in anticipation of my marriage to Matt, he has suggested we hire someone to help in the store. This will give the two of them a chance to make certain they work well together."

"Good. I'll have a carriage…"

"I plan to ride out there. I asked Maude if I could borrow one of the horses. I also wanted to get a pair of Matt's buckskins to make riding easier."

"I'm certain your father would prefer to see you in a dress. Since I need to return Spotted Pony's horse, you can pack the proper clothing along with some things Matt said he wanted to bring as gifts to the people since they recognized the danger you were in and imprisoned him."

Becky agreed. She knew the people liked the sugar cones she carried in the store as well as the trade blankets. It was the least she could do. These were things she could get at the trading post and replace once the danger was passed.

Chapter Fourteen

"You look worried, my brother." Soaring Eagle said when he found Hawk searching the horizon.

"It's a long journey. Anything could happen between here and the farm. What if Becky doesn't want to come. If she does, will a carriage be able to make it through the forest to the village?"

"You worry too much. I have met Becky when I went to the trading post. There is little that will stop her from getting here. Didn't you say she could ride a horse?"

"Of course she can. I have been teaching her how to ride. We often ride together, and she is turning into a good horsewoman."

"Then why the concern? She will be with your father."

Matt knew his brother was right, but his father was no longer a young man. Anything could happen to the two of them on the trail.

The thought crossed his mind when two riders along with a pack horse entered the village. He immediately recognized the riders as well as the pack horse. In the process of bringing Becky to the village, he was returning the horse Spotted Pony rode to exhaustion on his journey from the village to the farm.

He allowed Becky and his father to ride up to where he waited. He knew running to her would be unmanly in this male dominated society.

"I didn't know if you would come," he greeted her.

"It was hard for me to wait until Monday morning when your father was rested to leave. I wanted to ride out right after church. Was it terrible seeing him again?"

"It was hard. Running Deer's punishment was swift, but he did agree to allow him to see you one last time. I wanted you to come, but I prayed you would stay at the store. The people are anxious to meet you and grant you every courtesy. They have a lodge for travelers and have allowed me to stay there. I will leave it and move to the bachelor's lodge. As for Father, he is welcome in Running Deer's dwelling. It is only fitting as they are close to the same age. He stayed there while he rested before returning to the farm to see if you wanted to come and confront your father."

"I know I should see him, but it was you I came for. Do you think we could be married here? I don't want to let you out of my sight again."

"My mother and sisters would have a fit. They want to plan a grand wedding for us."

"They still can. Even though we are married in the village of your people, we can have a church wedding as soon as it can be arranged. I've been working on my wedding dress ever since you asked me to be your wife."

"I think it could be arranged, if that is what you want. Let's deal with your father first. Then I will talk with my brother's wife and see if she has something appropriate for you to wear."

~ * ~

While Hawk, as he was known in this village, went to talk to his brother, Becky went to the lodge she knew she would be sharing with the man she loved once they were married. She needed to change out of the buckskins she'd borrowed for the ride to the village and put on the dress she'd brought with her. Once she finished, she went in search of Matt.

As soon as she left the lodge she was met by a young woman. "I am Summer's Breeze," the woman said, introducing herself. "My husband is Soaring Eagle, brother of Hawk. My husband said to come to you with a dress that is fitting for you to be joined with Hawk."

"I met your husband when I was at the trading post. He resembles Hawk."

"That is a great compliment. We know Hawk now prefers to be called Matt. Only in this village he will always be known as Hawk."

Summer's Breeze held out a package wrapped in doe skin. "This was the dress I wore when I joined with Soaring Eagle. I would be honored if you would wear it for your mating with Hawk."

Becky opened the package and was in awe at the beauty of the white doeskin dress decorated with colorful beading. She recognized the beads as those available at the trading post.

"This is lovely. Are you certain you want me to wear it?"

"As I said, I would be honored to have you wear it. When you and Hawk are mated, it will be stored away for the daughter I hope to have in the future."

The young woman put her hand to her belly, indicating she was pregnant. If Becky's calculations were correct, there would be a little over a year in difference between the child Summer's Breeze carried and the little boy Matt told her was named Hunter.

Although Becky wanted children, she certainly didn't want them to be born so close together.

In the distance, she saw Matt coming toward her.

"Your father is ready to see you for the last time before he forfeits his life," Matt greeted her.

"Does he have to die?"

"I have no say in this and neither do you. Running Deer as well as Soaring Eagle saw evil in him. He is a threat to you, and he has dishonored the people of this village. He wanted them to do what went against everything they believe. Here, women are cherished. For someone to suggest the kidnapping and rape of a woman is an abomination."

Becky nodded. If her father were to live, she would always be looking over her shoulder to be certain he wasn't trying to do her harm.

Matt led her to a pole where her father was attached with a tether around his neck. Although his hands were free, the tether only allowed him short distance before it pulled tight. On either side of him stood a young brave who made certain he didn't try to escape his death sentence.

"Becky," he said, "tell them I'm your father and I love you."

"Love? You don't know the meaning of the word. The only reason you married my mother was because she was part owner of the store in Philadelphia. All you ever saw in her was the position she could give you. As for your so-called love for me, that is nonexistent as well. In Philadelphia, I became your bookkeeper and once we arrived here, you treated me more like hired help than a beloved daughter.

"I know what you asked these people to do. I also know none of them would ever think of doing such a thing. They cherish their women. They certainly don't ask someone to kidnap and rape them."

"You little bitch. It's what you deserve. From what I've heard, you're nothing more than a dried-up old maid. Any descent woman would have been married and tending to a house full of children by your age. A lady would never consider running a store. They don't have the mind for such a thing."

"You left me no other option than to run the store. I've shown a profit, even during the war when I was catering to the people who had no money but were able to barter for the supplies, they needed to keep their families alive. The things I took in were purchased by those who did have the money to do so.

"As for being an old maid, I was waiting for the man I loved to return from the war. Once your life is ended, the shaman will marry us. When we return to MacAfee farm, we will arrange for a Christian marriage. In that way we will honor both fathers who raised him."

"Are you saying you plan to marry the savage?"

"Whether he is called Hawk or Matt, he is my choice. I promise I will never tell our children what an evil man their grandfather was. I will only tell them you, like their grandmother, are dead. It doesn't matter how you die because the devil is waiting for you in hell. I will not grieve for you, since you have been dead to me for many years. This is my goodbye to you."

Becky turned on her heel and made her way back to the lodge where she had changed her clothes earlier. Whatever punishment her father was about to receive would be what he deserved.

When she arrived at the lodge, Summer's Breeze waited for her.

"Soaring Eagle told me how difficult seeing your father would be. He asked me to help you prepare for your mating with Hawk. The time for anger has passed. Now is when you should be getting ready to begin your new life with a great warrior and a respected breeder of horses."

Becky knew Summer's Breeze was right. Her future was with the man she loved, not the evil man who was her father. All she needed in her life was Matt and the family they knew they would have.

~ * ~

Like Becky, Matt had no desire to watch the execution of William. It was best if he knew only that the man was dead, not how he met the end of his life.

Even from Soaring Eagle's lodge, he could hear William's screams. He didn't have the decency to accept his death like an honorable man. Throughout the war, he'd seen the braves who followed him go to their deaths with dignity. William's death was one of a coward who was afraid to die.

"It is over," Soaring Eagle said when he entered the lodge.

"I could hear him pleading for his life."

"With this over, I have been told to help you dress for your mating to Becky. For the ceremony, Running Deer has given her a name fitting the people of our village. When she is here, she will be known as Brave Woman. It took a lot of courage for her to face her father today. Already, the women are preparing a feast to celebrate your mating."

Once inside Soaring Eagle's lodge, he was presented with the mating clothes his brother wore when he took Summer's Breeze as his wife. Dressed in the white doe skin suit with the fringe and beading on it, Matt reverted to being Hawk.

"Becky…ah Brave Woman had a good idea. It is only right that we should honor my father's people. We will honor Becky's white heritage as soon as a wedding can be arranged. Will you do me the honor of standing by my side for our mating?"

"There is nowhere else I would want to be."

~ * ~

Things seemed to be moving as fast as one of the MacAfee horses could run. Not only did Summer's Breeze help her dress for the mating ceremony, but the shaman came to the lodge.

"Running Deer wants you to be one with our people," the shaman said. "From now on, in this village, you will be known as Brave Woman. You earned your new name today when you faced the evil one."

Tears of appreciation formed in Becky's eyes. "I am honored to be accepted. Your people mean so much to Ma…Hawk."

"Now, Brave Woman, you need to finish preparing for the ceremony that will be held as the sun is setting."

When the shaman left the lodge, Becky turned to Summer's Breeze. "I didn't expect that."

"The name suits you. Hawk came by his name naturally but never has someone who is not of the people given such an honor. Naming someone is not taken without much thought. For now, we need to fix your hair in a style befitting one of our most honored women."

~ * ~

Caleb understood why Matt and Becky didn't want to witness William's execution. Even though the thought of watching a man die wasn't something he relished doing, he knew someone needed to be able to see William meet his end.

Like a hanging in the white community, it was evident the people were excited to witness the end of the evil doer's life. The execution grounds were filled with many men from the village.

Caleb stood to the back of the crowd and watched as William was led into the area and tethered to another pole. Before the activities of the execution began, the shaman stood before William and began to speak.

Although Caleb did not understand the ancient language the man spoke, it was evident he listed the crimes of the prisoner against the people of this village. He was certain William's intentions where Becky was concerned were also listed.

With each charge, the men stood silently, nodding in agreement to the sentence that was about to be carried out.

He watched in horror, as young braves attacked William with sharp knives. The death the man was about to experience would not be swift and painless. Although the punishment fit the crime, the brutality of it tore at Caleb's heart.

With each slice of the knives, William screamed in fear and pain. Matt once told him that when a true man of the people faced death, it was in silence. Only a coward would cry out in fear or pain.

William begged for them to either end his life quickly or let him go. Of course, Caleb knew neither request would be granted. It appears the torture went on for hours even though it was only a matter of less than half an hour from beginning until the cries ended and William forfeited his life.

With the execution ended, the man was stripped of his clothing and the body taken outside the village to become food for the scavengers who would pick the bones clean once night arrived. Already the vultures were gathering, hoping to get the first pick of the remains that had been left for them to feast upon.

~ * ~

Caleb watched the activity in the village. He'd just witnessed the execution of William now he awaited the mating of his son and Becky. It certainly wasn't the wedding he anticipated for his son, but he knew the proper Christian ceremony would take place once they returned to MacAfee farm.

When he saw his son emerging from Soaring Eagle's lodge, he was in awe of the beautiful white doeskin suit he wore. It was evident this was considered wedding finery among these people.

"You are a very handsome groom," he greeted his son.

"I hope Becky feels the same way. All of this is happening so quickly. Her father was just executed for his crimes against the people and now we're getting married."

"Perhaps after tonight you will be making us grandparents again."

"I doubt that. As much as I desire making her my wife in every way, I plan to abstain until after the ceremony at the church,"

"How does Becky feel about this?"

"She agrees with me. There are matters she needs to take care of before we can live as husband and wife. This ceremony is for the people and for us to be together tonight. She doesn't want to be alone, and I want to be able to protect her, even though the evil that brought her here can no longer hurt her."

"Your mother and sisters will be pleased with your decision. They have been making plans for when you decide to marry. As soon as we return to the farm, you can post the bonds at the church."

Soaring Eagle called Hawk away ceasing their conversation. Once the two young men walked away, so alike and yet so different, Running Deer came to Caleb's side.

"It is time for us to go to the place of mating," Running Deer said. "The sun is getting ready to set and the time for a mating has arrived."

Caleb nodded. "It is evident my son is well respected among your people. The ceremony that has been so quickly planned, attests to it."

"Hawk is a great warrior. His battles against the Red Coats will be told around the campfires, so his name is never forgotten. He and his brother, Soaring Eagle, will make their father proud. Their accomplishments helped not only our people, but also the Freedom

Fighters. Between you and Hunting Hawk, the boy has become a man. He will never be a leader here, as I know of his desire to return to MacAfee farm. Soaring Eagle's path in life is far different. In time, he will replace me as leader of our people, as I have no son to succeed me."

Caleb felt great pride not only in the son he raised, but Matt's half-brother who was destined for greatness. This new country would have good leaders.

~ * ~

Hawk gasped in awe at how beautiful the woman he was about to mate was. When she stepped into his view he drew in a breath. Here, in this village, she wasn't Becky, she was Brave Woman. The name suited her well and within the hour she would be his for all eternity.

Refraining from making her his, in every way, would be difficult, but they agreed it was for the best. Before they could live together as man and wife, she needed to turn the running of the store over to Stephen and find another person to help him with the day to day running of the store.

His duty was to build a house on the farm where they could raise the children he'd foreseen in their future.

The drums began to play as well as the flutes. The singers joined in the song of celebration. Slowly, Brave Woman walked toward him with Running Deer escorting her as though he was her father.

Although Hawk could understand the words the shaman spoke, he knew he would never remember them. All he knew was that after tonight, this beautiful woman would be his wife for the rest of his life.

Amid the ceremony, a vision assailed his mind. In it, he saw them living in the grand house his father built. The house he built for Brave Woman was now occupied by their son and they were old, with white hair. He interrupted it as a vision off the future.

When it came time for him to profess his love, the only words he could form were, "ever since we were children, we knew we were meant for each other. I promise to love you as much in our old age as I do on this day."

Brave Woman smiled at him and spoke from her heart. "Through the many years you were fighting the war, I waited for you. If need be,

I would have waited a lifetime to be your wife. I am honored to profess my love in front of the people who hold you in such high esteem."

Once the shaman blessed their joining, they turned to greet the people who gathered to wish them well in their union.

Beyond the ceremonial grounds, the wedding feast was held. With so little warning, it was amazing at how they were able to spread out such an abundance of food.

The people embraced the white woman who had been adopted by their chief. Hawk was proud of his wife. Not only was she successful in the white word, but she was also respected by the people who he considered his other family.

~ * ~

The lodge where Becky changed her clothes looked much different for the wedding night. Thick furs made up the bed meant to share for their first night as man and wife. Around the interior of the lodge, fall flowers gave off a heady scent and added to the beauty of the area.

"Are you sure you want to wait?" she asked before they took off their wedding finery.

"I'm not sure of anything, but in the eyes of God I want our first lovemaking to occur after we have been joined together in the church. For tonight, I will be content to hold you in my arms and kiss all your fears away."

"I have no fears. This is what I want, what I've wanted since the first day I saw you."

"In that case I will claim everything, except for your virginity. I want everything proper when Thomas joins us together in the eyes of God."

Chapter Fifteen

Leaving the Indian village was bittersweet. Here was where Becky's father forfeited his life because of his evil plans concerning her. It was also where she promised herself to Matt and accepted the new name given to her by Chief Running Deer.

Ahead of her, she knew there was much to do before they could be married in the eyes of God. The first thing she would have to do would be to promote Stephen to the manager of the store and to hire someone to work as storekeeper with him. She hoped he had an idea of an ideal candidate he could work well with.

"What is the first thing you plan to do when we return to the farm?" she asked as they rode side by side.

"I want to go into the village and talk to Thomas about posting the bans for our wedding. After that, I know there are new foals I want to check out."

"I'm pleased you put me before your beloved horses," she teased. "To be honest, I was thinking about getting things settled at the store. Of course, once that is done, I need to finish my wedding dress. Before I came out to the Indian village, the lace I ordered to finish the project came in."

"I have been talking to my father, and he says we can stay with them until our house is built. With all the new people moving into the village, it might take a while to get it finished."

Becky didn't know how she felt about living in Maude and Caleb's home. She wasn't comfortable knowing his father-in-law and mother-in-law would be sleeping just down the hall from the bedroom they would share until their home was built, and they could move in. On the other hand, she didn't want to have to wait any longer than necessary to be Matt's wife in every sense of the word.

~ * ~

It broke Matt's heart to know Becky was living above the store. He should have made her his wife once they were joined by the shaman in the village that had become his second home.

He was checking the horses in the far pasture when he saw a rider coming toward the farm. Thinking the man was a horse buyer, he urged his horse forward to greet the visitor.

"I'm looking for MacAfee farm," the man said, his voice laced with a heavy Scottish burr.

"You've been on the farm for the last mile. Can I help you?"

"I don't deal with hired men. I only want to speak with your master."

"I am Matthew MacAfee."

"I was told my uncle Caleb ran this farm."

The man's attitude rubbed Matt the wrong way. "Caleb is my father. He's at the house. I'll gladly take you to meet him."

"I never thought someone with the name of MacAfee would take up with an Indian birth. Of course, I doubt he had much choice in women."

"Caleb MacAfee is my father in love. He and his wife, Maude, raised me when my mother was killed. She lived long enough to give life to me. It's a long story and one best for my father to tell."

"I'm certain it is. I won't talk to anyone other than my uncle."

"Since you know my name, what is yours?"

"Not that it's any of your business, but my name is Michael MacAfee."

Matt wondered why this pompous young man was here. He'd heard the man's name only once before and what his father told him was not flattering.

"It's a pleasure to make your acquaintance, Michael MacAfee. I know my father will be grateful to have family visiting."

"I wish I could saw the same. I don't like to have dealings with inferiors, especially savages."

Matt cringed at the offensive name he'd endured throughout his life. Even when the Red Coats called him The Savage, he had not felt it as a badge of honor. It was more like a name given someone to be feared by his fight for freedom from British rule.

The remainder of the ride back to the house was in silence. Instead of relaxing at the house, Caleb was coming from the stable.

"You have a guest, Father," Matt announced. "He says he wants to talk to you because you are his uncle. He told me his name is Michael MacAfee."

He could almost see the hair on the back of his father's neck stand out as anger flashed from his green eyes.

"Welcome, Michael," Caleb greeted their visitor with a false sincerity in his voice. "How is my brother, Sean?"

"He is a bastard," Michael spat. "I went to him for a job after my father took his own life. He treated me like one of the stableboys when I was able to train the horses."

"That is not the way I heard the story. Sean told me what he couldn't tolerate were your lazy ways. I pray you have learned a valuable lesson since then. Considering you have come here; I must assume you want something from me."

"According to my father and Uncle Sean, you have no sons, at least none that are of your making. I've come to take over MacAfee Farm and keep the name and the property in the proper relations. It would be a shame to leave it in the hands of people with no blood relationship to the family."

"In that case, you've made a long journey for nothing. The farm will be managed by my son, Matt. Not only is he an excellent manager of my property but he is a war hero."

"A savage as a war hero and heir to all of this?" Michael emphasized his question with a swipe of his hand. "Everyone knows the natives are little more than animals."

"You have no say in this. As far as I can see, you are little more than a pompous popinjay. What I do with my property and my family is none of your business. I can't believe Sean sent you here for any reason than to be rid of you. As far as I'm concerned, you are no better than your father. I know he was my older brother, but he was a drunk who lost everything our father gave him. If either of you were responsible landowners, you would be a wealthy man. I will not have you ruining what I built when there was nothing left for me in Scotland."

"You can't treat me like that. I am family."

"You are little more than a spoiled child. Go back to Scotland. There is no place for you in this new country."

"I-I can't. Uncle Sean made it clear I was not to return. It isn't fair."

"If that's how you feel, make your way north to Canada. I'm

certain the British will be more than happy to have someone in their midst who is good with horses. God knows they could use the help."

"Caleb, do we have company?" Maude said as she stepped out onto the porch.

"It's only Michael MacAfee and he was just leaving."

"Where are your manners, Caleb? It's getting late, and the evening meal is almost ready to be served. I will have no problem in setting another place at the table. God knows we have enough room for a visitor to spend the night, so he can be on his way tomorrow morning when he is rested."

"An Englishwoman?" Michael questioned. "Did you stoop so low as to marry an English bitch?"

"It's none of your business who I married. Maude is the love of my life. She knows exactly who and what you are, yet she has offered you food and shelter. Everyone knows your mother was a harlot and it is possible Eric was not your father.

"Although I don't agree with my wife, I will honor her wishes. You are welcome to share our evening meal and spend the night. I do expect you to be gone first thing in the morning. I don't care where you go, if it is not to the village where my other children live and work. My son, Matt, will escort you in whatever direction you plan to go."

~ * ~

Michael certainly didn't expect the greeting he received from his uncle. Damn Sean for portraying him in a bad light.

He'd been certain Caleb would welcome him with open arms and turn over MacAfee farm to him. Throughout the long voyage from Scotland, he dreamed of running the farm and profiting from the reputation his uncle's horses carried. Certainly, the man had good help who could run the farm, while he maintained the position of lord of the manor. The profits would easily support the lifestyle he enjoyed. With the war ending, he was sure there were widows who would willingly give him the pleasure he desired, while he indulged in drinking and gambling, he so enjoyed.

With Uncle Caleb's ultimatum, those plans dissolved like fog that vanished when the morning sun burned it off. He would have to come up with a new plan for his life. In no way would he be going to

Canada, where the British fought to maintain the land and defeat the French.

On the ship, he'd met several young men who were talking about going to the untamed frontier to the west. At the time he thought they were crazy, but his uncle gave him no other choice.

They formed a friendship of sorts. Perhaps he could join up with others like them and head west.

~ * ~

Matt agreed with his father's opinion of Michael MacAfee. The man annoyed him as soon as they met earlier in the day. Rather than stay at the house and listen to the conversation between his father and Michael, he left to check on the new foal that was born early that morning.

"She's a strong little filly," John told him when he entered the stable.

Matt knew there was no need to check on the filly that was suckling on his mother's tit. The horses were in capable hands with John as the head groom. Since his return from the war, they'd formed not only a good working relationship, but also a friendship he knew would last for the rest of their lives.

He returned to the house that was being built for when he and Becky were properly married. Men from the farm as well as from town worked on the construction. It wouldn't be the grand house his father built when he first arrived in the new world. It was a more modest two-story dwelling. One Matt designed himself.

"I thought I'd find you here," his father said. "Your mother sent me down to get you for the evening meal. Before we go up to the house, we need to talk."

"Does this have anything to do with Michael?"

"It has everything to do with that man. I know you are planning the wedding, but I need to have you take him as far away from this farm as possible. I must talk to your mother about this, but she has a friend up by the Ohio River Valley. She us lived in the settlement several years ago. She met a farmer who was interested in going west and homesteading there. He bought some horses from me so he could start a horse breeding operation.

"Over the years, your mother and Peggy have remained in touch. We will send a message to Ohio. In the meantime, I want you to take Michael there."

"What if they won't accept him?" Matt inquired.

"If Peggy and her husband want nothing to do with him, you can leave him to his own devices. If he succeeds, so be it. If not, I'm washing my hands of him."

Matt had doubts about escorting his cousin to Ohio. Rather than voicing them, he followed his father up to the house. As they entered the door yard, he saw Becky's carriage. It didn't come as a surprise, as she came out for the evening meal every night since their mating ceremony at the Indian village.

"I was beginning to think you and your father got lost," his mother greeted him.

"We had something to talk about."

Rather than continuing the conversation with his mother, Matt went to Becky's side to escort her to the table.

"I heard this lovely lady is going to be your wife," Michael said when they took their seats. "Someone as beautiful as Miss Becky deserves better than the likes of you."

Before Matt could respond, Becky spoke up. "I've only just met you, but what Matt and I do with our lives should be none of your business. I waited through all the long years of the war for him to come home and make me his wife."

"From what I hear, he fought with the Indians during the war. You must know they're little more than a step above the animals. I'm told they mate with any woman who crosses their path. Are you content to be married to someone like that, when you could have me. In Scotland I would have been the Lord of the Manor, if my father hadn't drunk and gambled away the farm, I would have been set for life."

"This isn't preferred table talk," Maude said. "It's time for grace so we can eat before everything gets cold."

Matt was so proud of Becky for standing up to Machael when he made nasty comments about their upcoming marriage. If she hadn't defended their union, he would have been tempted to take the man outside and beat some sense into him.

Instead of saying anything about the confrontation, Matt folded his hands and bowed his head in prayer. While his father prayed to thank God for the bountiful food that graced the table and the hands that prepared it. Silently, Matt prayed for the patience to take Michael to Ohio without killing the man.

~ * ~

Michael's overnight stay turned into almost a week. Matt convinced his father he would feel more secure with Soaring Eagle joining him for the journey. Although he knew he was going into hostile territory, he feared Michael more than the Shawnee who lived in the area.

"Are you so afraid of me you had to bring your savage friend to protect you?" Michael asked when Soaring Eagle arrived at the farm.

"We are going into Shawnee territory. Soaring Eagle and I have had dealings with the Shawnee. It is best we go together to protect you and get you safe passage. To make things clear, Soaring Eagle is my half-brother. We share the same father. If he were the one making this journey, I would be honored to go with him as well. We fought against the British together and if necessary, we will fight together to keep you safe."

Matt cringed at the half truth. Soaring Eagle was coming with them to protect Michael against Matt's temper, not the Shawnee.

When Michael was out of earshot, Soaring Eagle motioned for Matt to walk with him. "Who is the man we are taking to Ohio?" he asked in their native language.

Matt explained the relationship between his father and Michael. He went into detail about the stories he'd heard about the dealings the MacAfee family had with the man leading to his banishment to the new world.

"I can't believe he would expect your father to give him title to what has been promised to you."

"Neither could my father. His suggestion that he take over MacAfee farm wasn't the only thing he suggested. He has been making nasty suggestions to Becky ever since he got here. Thank God she has been able to stand up for herself. She has managed the store for many years. She knows how to handle someone as pompous as Michael."

"I have a feeling you did not ask me to accompany you because you fear the Shawnee."

"You are too perceptive. In truth you are here to protect him from

112

me. I fear he will push me too far and I might kill him. I also don't want to return to the farm alone. I will enjoy your company once we leave him to his destiny."

"What do you know of this friend of your mother's?"

"Not much. I do know they were good friends and I'm certain Mother warned her about Michael when she sent the letter saying we would be taking him to their farm. He is so full of himself, I am certain he won't be receptive to working as a stable boy or even a groom. He might stay with them until they kick him out and leave him to his own devices."

~ * ~

The next morning, Matt was up early, as was Soaring Eagle. Even though they were ready to leave shortly after sunrise, the sun was already high in the sky when Michael finally joined them.

"I thought we agreed to get an early start," Matt said.

"It is early. My God, Matt, the sun is hardly up. I have always liked to sleep late."

"On this journey, you will not be able to indulge in such a pleasure. We came this way during the war and there is a large forest to traverse. Because of the thickness of the trees, evening comes early. To make good time, we will be leaving shortly after sunrise each day."

Michael scowled, but Matt didn't care. Either him or Soaring Eagle would wake the man each morning to get on the trail as early as possible.

Once Michael finished his breakfast, Matt insisted they begin the journey to Ohio. Knowing the area as well as he did, he purposely took the most treacherous route,

"When are we going to stop for dinner?" Michael complained.

"We will be eating as we ride," Matt replied, as Soaring Eagle reached into a pack tied to the side of his horse and produced a stick of dried meat and fruit.

"You call this eating?"

"When you're on the trail, you must take advantage of as much daylight as possible," Soaring Eagle replied. "Once we make camp for the night my brother and I will go hunting for game for the evening meal."

"Game?" Mchael asked, wrinkling his nose in disgust.

"Hopefully we will be able to get a rabbit or a fat squirrel."

Matt was glad his two traveling companions rode behind him. Had they been riding side by side, Michael would see the smile Matt displayed in place of the laughter he was forcing himself to hide. There had been days during the war, when one or two rabbits kept the war party from starving. Living off the land was something his birth people did for generations.

Making camp in the forest came earlier than if he'd been on the farm. Each of them brought a tent with them.

As Matt could have predicted, Michael complained bitterly about their accommodation for the night.

"Isn't there an inn somewhere close by?"

"You aren't in Scotland, Michael," Matt replied. "This is the frontier. The country is wild, and no one has built an inn for the few travelers who might come this way. Be glad my father supplied you with a tent to stay in while we are on the trail. While Soaring Eagle is out hunting for our evening meal, I will help you set up your tent and get a fire started."

"A fire? Won't that attract the hostiles?"

"They already know we are here. If they want to attack it won't be because we have lit a campfire."

Matt knew there was no reason to worry, since it would be at least another day before they rode into Shawnee territory. It was meant to put Michael on the defensive. It was something his father taught him at an early age. Relying on one's instincts could be the difference between life and death.

By the time their camp was set up and a fire blazed, Soaring Eagle return with a fat rabbit for the evening meal. It didn't take long for Matt to skin the rabbit and put it on a spit.

"I see living at the farm hasn't dulled your skill with a knife or cooking over an open fire," Soaring Eagle said.

"I must admit although the meals my mother serves at her table I miss catching and roasting my meal."

"Certainly, Aunt Maude must have packed something for us to eat," Michael complained.

"In the heat of the day anything she would have sent might spoil. Although she suggested it, I insisted we would be able to eat off the land. Father agreed with me. He knows how my birth people live, and they do not go to the store for supplies. They do not raise animals for meat. The men are hunters, and the women tend to the crops. Our birth father was the leader of the hunters and taught us the same skills. On this journey, you will not starve. You must adjust to eating what we can provide for you."

Along with the rabbit, Soaring Eagle produced some edible plants. Matt washed them in the creek and retrieved the cooking pot his mother insisted he take with them. It didn't take long for the water to boil the cooking plants to add to their meal.

"How do I know you aren't planning to poison me?" Michael asked.

"Poison you? I've cooked you a meal, one my brother and I plan to share why would we poison it?"

"You eat first. If you eat it, so will I. I don't put anything past you. It's evident you don't like me."

"I don't have to like you to deliver you safely to my mother's friend's farm. I could have allowed you to find your own way, but I respect my parents enough that I would never do anything like that."

~ * ~

The next morning, Matt and Soaring Eagle were up and ready to travel before the sun rose above the eastern horizon. In contrast, Michael slept peacefully, his snores breaking the morning silence. Even the waking sounds of the birds and small animals could not drown out the annoying sound.

"When should we wake him?" Soaring Eagle asked.

"I'm planning to do so right now. I told him before we left the farm, I expected him to be ready to ride early when we were on the trail. The longer this journey lasts the more danger we are in from the Shawnee."

"If my memory serves me correctly, we should be close to their village when we camp for the night. Once we've eaten the evening meal, I plan to ride to the village and speak with the elders. You know they hold you in high esteem."

"Until we stop for the night, we are in danger from the young scouts who know nothing of who we are or that we fought with their fathers and brothers during the war. I will be more comfortable once you have ridden to their village."

"In that case, I will leave as soon as you and Michael are on the trail. You know I can make better time by myself. If all goes well, I will be waiting for you in the Shawnee village. If not, I will plead with the elders to be able to return and warn you to keep your distance where they are concerned."

Matt agreed with his brother. The sooner he contacted the elders of the Shawnee village, the safer the remainder of the journey would be.

Soaring Eagle was preparing to leave when Matt woke Michael from his sound sleep. From his tent, Michael grumbled at being awaken so early in the morning.

"I told you before we left the farm that we would be leaving early when we were on this journey. My brother and I have been up and ready to leave since before the sun crested the horizon. I am ready to ride, and I suggest you get ready as well."

"What about breakfast? Am I to go hungry?"

"You can eat on the trail. The day is already well underway. If we hope to make it to the Shawnee village by nightfall, we need to leave now."

"I need to relieve myself."

"I understand your need. As soon as you are finished, I will have food ready for you to eat once we are on the trail. We left enough of the rabbit for you to enjoy for your breakfast."

"Speaking of we, where is that savage brother of yours?" Michael asked, relieving himself without the modesty of doing so in the forest.

"Be careful who you call a savage. Even the smallest child in his village knows better than to relieve himself where it is offensive to others. My brother has gone ahead to the Shawnee village for ensure our safety."

"I thought you said we were in their territory yesterday. Are you a liar?"

"Because we were in their territory doesn't mean we were close to their village. They claim a large territory as their own. The village is in the middle of the area. Now get on your horse. I'm ready to ride."

Although Michael grumbled about having to leave and eat his breakfast on the trail, he did as Matt told him.

Throughout the day, Matt listened to all of Michael's complaints about having to ride all day without stopping for anything other than to relieve themselves and have something to eat.

"I don't know how you can consider yourself the lord of the manor," Michael commented as they mounted their horses to ride throughout the afternoon. "A gentleman doesn't push himself like this. He would ride at a more leisurely pace."

"As I've told you before, you are no longer in Scotland. Here there is no such thing as the lord of the manor. My father works as hard as any of the stable boys or grooms. He is no better than anyone who works for him. When he first came here, he built the farm with his own hands. The story goes, that before he began to build the farm, he went to my birth people to ask permission to build on the land he'd been granted by the British. He lords nothing over anyone. He is a well-respected breeder of fine horses."

"My Uncle Sean would be embarrassed to think his one surviving brother is little more than a commoner. For generations, the MacAfee's have been considered only a step down from Scottish royalty. I thought…"

"You thought wrong. I've read Father's letters from Uncle Sean, and they do not sound as though he is embarrassed by my father. Instead, he is proud of the accomplishments Father has made in this new world, this new country."

If Matt thought he'd silenced is Scottish cousin, he was wrong. The man kept up a constant conversation about how miserable he was on this journey. Rather than arguing further, he let Michael rant without answering. His thoughts of Becky helped him to tune out Michael's irritating voice.

~ * ~

Soaring Eagle didn't envy his brother for the journey today. He'd had enough of Michael's complaints, and they'd only been on the trail for one day.

He could smell the Shawnee village before he saw it in the distance. The aroma coming from the cooking fires made his mouth water. Even though he wouldn't ask for them to provide his midday meal, he knew the hunting in the area would be good. It was possible he would be able to bring down a deer to share with the people he needed to ask for protection.

It came as no surprise when six braves rode up to meet him. "You are not of our people," one of the young braves said, his voice laced with anger.

"I have come to see the elders. I am Soaring Eagle, and I come from people to the south. I come in peace and wish only for safe passage."

"I do not know you," the oldest of the braves said. "For now, you are our prisoner."

Soaring Eagle willingly held out his hands to be bound and handed over the reins of his horse. He could tell none of the young men were more than fourteen winters old. Once he met with the elders, things would be different.

He held onto the mane of his horse for support as the young men rode at almost a gallop calling with whoops of victory. For them, he knew, the capture of an interloper was a great honor.

Chief Rushing Water came out of his lodge to greet the young men and share in their victory.

"Soaring Eagle, to what do we owe the honor of you coming to our village?"

"I come as a friend. I seek safe passage for The Savage and a white man named Michael MacAfee."

"I see you as a prisoner of our young braves."

"They were doing as they should. You can be proud of them," Soaring Eagle said, holding out his hands to be untied.

"Tell me of this man named Michael," Rushing Water said, as he escorted Soaring Eagle to his lodge. "Why is The Savage bringing him through our territory?"

Soaring Eagle sat at the fire and accepted the bowl of stew, and Rushing Water's tea offered him, before he began to tell his story.

"I know of Frank Stewart and his wife Peggy. They are good people and treat the land as I have heard Caleb MacAfee does. From what you have said about this man. Michael, he will not be with them for any length of time. I will give Michael and The Savage safe passage, but should he be banned from the Stewart farm, I will not vouch for his safety."

"I completely understand. If I were in your position, I would think the same way. My brother feels this is an obligation to the white father who raised him. I feel it is an obligation to my brother. I have only spent less than two days with this man and if my brother hadn't given his word, I would kill him myself."

Rushing Water laughed. "Not much has changed in you since we fought against the Red Coats during the war. Do you know where your brother planned to camp tonight?"

"We weren't sure. I'm certain he is taking the same trail I used to get here. I do know he will push forward to get as close to your village as possible. I do worry about him pushing himself to the limit. As I'm certain you know, he was wounded during the last battle he fought in the war. Unfortunately, he does not have the strength for such an undertaking."

"I did hear about his wound. I grieved to think he had been injured, but I rejoiced to think the Red Coats were unable to capture him. I will get you a fresh horse and the two of us will ride out to find him. He need not make a camp for the night. He is welcome in our village. I'm certain he will appreciate a hot meal that he doesn't have to hunt to provide."

~ * ~

Although Michael considered himself an expert horseman, Matt knew the nonstop ride was tiring him out. He knew he could feel his strength draining from his body. Even though he fought his injury for over a year, he still had to admit he needed to rest.

In the distance he saw Rushing Water riding next to his brother. At least they wouldn't be taken prisoner. During the war he and Rushing Water had become good friends. Had they not been granted safe passage, it would have been a war party coming to meet them.

"Hawk, it is a pleasure to see you, my friend," Rushing Water said in greeting.

"I never expected to come this far north, but I made a promise to my father."

"That makes you a good son. Your birth father would be proud of you as a man. Soaring Eagle tells me of your upcoming marriage to the woman you spoke of often when we rode together. He also told me; you were married in the old way. That should be enough of a joining. I do not understand the need for a second marriage. I do understand your need to please your woman. Even though I heard about her from your brother, I have heard other things about her. You are blessed to have a woman who is both brave and intelligent."

"You always had a way with words, Rushing Water. Thank you for speaking in your language so that Michael does not understand what you are saying. He has met Becky and knows nothing of the joining we participated in while in the village of my birth. He also doesn't know why we were in the village together or the name of the people Running Deer gave her before the ceremony."

"Your brother told me about it. I can't imagine the strength it took for her to stand up to the father who wanted to do unthinkable things to her. Had it been me, I would have exultated him myself. For tonight, you will be able to rest and eat your fill from our women's cooking pots."

~ * ~

Matt relaxed against the fur lined backrest. How much harm could Michael bring about for one night. By this time tomorrow, they would be at the Stewart farm, and he could make his way back home to Becky.

A commotion in the village woke Matt from a sound sleep. Soaring Eagle was also awake. Matt looked at the furs where Michael had been lying before they went to sleep and found them empty.

"Where's Michael," he asked his brother.

"I don't know. He was here when I went to sleep. I have a bad feeling the commotion has something to do with Michael."

Matt knew what his brother was saying. He worried about the same thing where Mchael was concerned. He remembered how he practically suggested he wanted to take Becky to his bed.

After pulling on their buckskins, he and Soaring Eagle left the lodge. By the large fire in the center of the village, they saw Michael being held tightly by two braves.

"What's going on?" Matt asked Running Water.

"He tried to rape one of the maidens. Had she not called out, he would have violated her. For tonight he will be held until guard if you leave in the morning. I will not have such atrocities in my village. I know you and your brother are honorable men, but if this one crosses my path again, he will pay for what he did tonight with his life."

Matt agreed with his friend. His people were taught not to rape women. It was no wonder Sean MacAfee banished Michael from Scotland. If his actions here were any indication of how he lived his life, he would have banished the man as well.

He knew of the unmarried men who went to the rooms above the tavern to pay for the services of the women who made their living by lying with men who weren't their husbands. The very thought of such actions sickened him as he knew it sickened his white father. What transpired between a man and a woman were for the marriage bed, not because someone felt as though they needed to be sexually satisfied to be considered a man.

"Tell them I was just being a man, Matt," Michel pleaded.

"I don't consider you an honorable man. I don't even think it's right to call you a man when you are nothing more than the animal you accuse my people of being. I will take you to the Stewart farm tomorrow and forget I ever met you. Either you work and earn an honest living or may God have mercy on your soul."

Matt turned on his heel and left Michael with his guards. He knew the man would be imprisoned on the far fringes of the village and his night would not be a restful one.

~ * ~

Early the next morning, they left Rushing Water's village. Matt didn't speak a word to Michael, and the man was unusually quiet during the ride.

How am I going to tell the Stewarts about Michael's action in Rushing Water's village? Knowing what he is guilty of, will they even hire him? If they don't what will I do with the man. I know Pa made it perfectly clear he wants the man nowhere near MacAfee farm.

They were surprised at how close the Stewarts lived to Rushing Water's village. By evening they were riding up to the door yard.

Peggy Stewart met them as they dismounted. "Matthew, it's good to see you. The last time I saw your mother, you were no more than three or four years old. You've grown into a handsome young man."

"Thank you, Mrs. Stewart," Matt began.

"Now, none of that Mrs. Stwart thing. You are to call me Peggy. I've known your mother long enough that it's only fitting. I take it the young Scotsman you have with you is Michael. Who is this other handsome young man."

Matt introduced his brother to Peggy and Frank who had joined them. Before going into the house, he felt it necessary to warn them about Michael. Getting them alone he began to tell them what transpired at Rushing Water's village.

"You don't need to go any further," Frank interrupted. "Last night Rushing Water sent one of the men to warn us about this man. That, added to the letter from your mother, means we have been warned. If he doesn't work out here, I will make certain he doesn't trespass on the land of Rushing Water's people or make his way to MacAfee farm. I will personally take him to Canada where the British can deal with him."

"That is what I wanted to do before we left home, but Mother insisted he be given a chance to turn his life around under your guidance."

Frank laughed at Matt's statement. "If the man knows what is good for him, he will work well for us. Should I take him to Canada, the British will not look upon him kindly. For now, Peggy has supper ready, and I know you need to rest. Stay with us tonight and tomorrow return to Rushing Water's village. He also worries about your need to rest before you begin your journey back to your home. You may not know it, but there are many people of both races who hold you in high esteem and want nothing more than for you to regain the strength this journey has drained from your body."

Chapter Sixteen

Soaring Eagle was anxious to return to his family. As much as he disliked leaving his brother in the Shawnee village, he knew Hawk needed the rest. Rushing Water assured him Hawk would be well cared for until he regained the strength for the journey back to MacAfee farm. Once he was able to return Rushing Water promised to send some of his braves with him so he wouldn't be making the journey alone.

After the second day Soaring Eagle prepared to leave the village. The night before Hawk make him promise to stop at Brave Woman's store as well as MacAfee farm to give them the details of the delay in Hawk returning home.

At Rushing Water's insistence, two young braves rode to within a day's ride of the white village to assure his safety and give him companionship. The braves were older than the ones who took him as a captive, days earlier. Like Soaring Eagle, they were expert hunters giving them enough in common that they were compatible traveling companions.

"You and your brother are a legend for the battles you fought in the war," Standing Bear said. "What was it like to fight side by side with the man the Red Coats called The Savage?"

"How does one describe his brother? Even though our mothers were different and we were raised in separate places, we shared something that cannot be put into words. Recently we have learned one of our ancestors was a great shaman. Although we are not trained in that area, we both have visions of the future. During the war, those visions served us well."

Soaring Eagle could tell his traveling companions were in awe of the stories he relayed to them. To him, the visions he and his brother experienced were as natural as breathing. Never had he thought they would be of interest to anyone other than themselves.

~ * ~

Although Becky understood the need for Matt to take Michael as far away from MacAfee farm as possible, she worried about him having to travel through Shawnee territory. Many of the new people who settled in the are told stories of the tribe who frightened them. Their stories were used to frighten children into behaving properly.

The scheduled day of the wedding came and went with no sign of Matt returning. She worried the strain of the journey was too much for him. Less than a week before the arrival of Michael at MacAfee farm they'd returned from the Indian village. She knew the stress of the time he spent with his brother, and the others of his birth people were draining for him. Especially with her father facing a death sentence for what he planned concerning her welfare.

She was beginning to wish they'd consummated their marriage on the night of their joining. If they had, she might be carrying his child and have a part of him if he didn't return from the long journey he'd embarked upon.

The bell above the door of the store signaled a customer had arrived. Weeks ago, she would have hurried to see who her customer could be. Instead, she stayed in the back office working on the books detailing the transactions of the past week. Stephen or his new helper, Zack Adams, could take care of the needs of their customers.

"There's an Indian here. He says he wants to talk to you," Zack said interrupting her internal thoughts of Matt.

"Did he tell you, his name?"

From the fear on Zack's face, she could tell he was so terrified, even if the Indian did tell him his name, the man wouldn't remember.

"He said something about who he was, but I-I can't remember what he said."

"That's alright. I'll be right out."

As much as she wanted the man who waited for her to be Matt, she knew it wasn't him. In her heart she knew something was wrong. Her suspicions were confirmed when she saw Soaring Eagle waiting for her.

He took her hand in his. "Hawk sent me to tell you he has been delayed in returning to you."

"Is he hurt?"

"Not in the way you think. The journey was stressful, and I could see his strength draining. Frank Stewart insisted he rest and so did Rushing Water, the chief of the Shawnee. Everyone thought it was best if he rests with Rushing Water's people, away from where Michael was staying."

"How long before he will be able to return home?" she relieved for the first time since Matt left to take Michael to the Stewart's farm.

"Everyone agrees he should rest for a week. When he is ready to travel, Rushing Water will be sending two of his braves to escort him home. He did the same for me, so I would not have to travel alone."

"Where are they? Should I prepare something for them to eat?"

"We parted company yesterday. They needed to get back to their families and I did not want to frighten the residents with the presence of two strangers. Although I enjoyed the company on the journey, I needed this past day to prepare to speak with you and the MacAfee's."

"I thank you for coming to see me first. I know Caleb and Maude will be relieved to hear your news about Matt. I've spoken to Calbe several times in the past few days, and he blames self for insisting Matt escort Michael to Ohio."

"Speaking of Michael, what has happened with him?"

"We spent a night with the Shawnee, and he tried to violate one of the maidens. He cannot return to their village under the penalty of death. We left him at the Stewart farm. Frank has promised that if things do not work out for him, he will personally take him to Canada and turn him over to the British. He says the hatred between the Scots, and the British is well known. He will not have an easy life under their rules. If he is as good with the horses as he says, he will be an asset to the Stewarts."

"I hope no one here ever has to deal with that man again," Becky said,

"I agree with you. Now that I have put your mind at ease I must leave to speak with Caleb."

"At least let me provide you with a meal before you leave."

She searched Soaring Eagle's face to try and see his reaction to her suggestion. She knew he would be on the trail for at least the next two days, and she couldn't allow him to ride without something to eat and at least a couple of hours to rest.

"You are very generous Brave Woman. As much as I want to be on the trail to go to my home, it has been several hours since I ate my morning meal. Being in your village, I have no means to be able to hunt. I will accept your offer."

"Will you be back for our wedding?"

"I have spent much time on the trail already. I need time with my family. Hawk and I talked about my attendance but decided I was with him when you first joined. The ceremony, of which you speak is for his white family. I would feel as out of place as I am sure Caleb felt at your joining. He knows I will be with you in spirit if not physical form."

Becky understood her brother-in-law's need to get his life back to normal with his family. She knew Matt understood this need as well.

~ * ~

Maude fretted over not only the absence of her youngest son, but the depression her husband was experiencing for asking Matt to take Michael away from the farm concerned her as well. As she had at the end of the war, she sat a third plate on the table for each meal.

Rather than checking on his beloved horses, Caleb spent his days on the porch scanning the horizon for a glimpse of Matt and his brother to return from the journey he sent them on. She was beginning to worry about him as he seemed to age almost overnight.

The chill of the winter winds filled the air and came with more concern than usual. While the horses thrived under John's care, she still wanted her son home.

"Come out here, Maude," Caleb called as she finished cleaning her kitchen after the noon meal.

Excitement quickly turned to dread, as she saw Soaring Eagle riding into the door yard alone.

"My son," she pleaded, "has something happened to my son?"

"It is not as you think," Soaring Eagle said as he dismounted. "Nothing has happened to my brother other than the exhaustion he has experienced ever since he was wounded in the war. The chief of the Shawnee as well as Frank Stewart insisted, he should rest before returning to his home and the woman he loves. I stopped to see Brave Woman before I came here. It was Hawk's request that I do so. With my obligation to my brother fulfilled, I am anxious to return to my home and my family."

"You too need to rest before you return to your family," Maude insisted. "A few more hours will make little difference. Spend the night with us and begin again tomorrow morning when you and your horse have had time to rest."

Indecision radiated from Soaring Eagle's eyes.

"Maude is right," Caleb said. "We owe you more than we can ever repay for everything you have done for us and our son. Allow us to compensate you with our hospitality and one of my best horses. You may have your pick of mare of stallion. It will add to your herd and be but a small payment toward what we owe you."

Soaring Eagle's shoulders slumped. It was entirely evident he was torn between accepting their offer and riding hard to get back to his home.

"You are right," he finally said. "This has been a long journey and the thought of resting for even a few hours outweighs my need to return to my family. I will accept your offer as a boon to my brother. He would expect nothing less than that I tell you of our journey and everything that transpired since we left your farm."

Maude smiled. She knew it was hard for this proud warrior to show any weakness. By waiting until morning, he would get the rest he needed and have his pick of one of Caleb's prize horses.

She could also see a difference in her husband. For the first time since Michael arrived at the farm, he was excited about something other than his concerns for their son.

~ * ~

"Much has happened since we left the farm," Soaring Eagle said as he and Caleb walked through the stable assessing each of the horses. "I know your woman wants to know everything, but there are things women shouldn't have to hear."

"What do you mean?" Caleb inquired.

"The man was an annoyance from the minute we left on the journey. The first day on the journey, he complained nonstop. He didn't like eating as he rode, nor did he approve of the meal we provided for him when we stopped for the night.

"By the next morning, I feared for my temper as well as that of my brother. At Hawk's insistence, I rode ahead of them to the Shawnee village. When we reunited, Hawk told me of how the man relieved himself without seeking out the privacy of the forest. Even the youngest child in my village knows better than to do something like that. Both men and women go to the area designed for such private moments not only for modesty, but out of respect for the people.

"We spent one night with the Shawnee and during that time Michael tried to take one of their women by force. Only her screams saved her from being violated by him. To think they call us savages when they are the ones who feel they can take what they want without asking. I will admit our young men take women to their furs before they are joined. At my joining, my mate, Summer's Breeze, carried my child, but she wasn't taken against her will. Had she protested, I would have been willing to wait until we were joined before I made her mine in every way."

"You have seen the worst in the whites. Between Michael and William, your people have been subjected to men with no morals. I was selfish enough not to want to have him anywhere around my family. I put the obligation on my son. I should have known better. I know Matt is not up to the journey I sent him on. He was right to ask you to accompany him."

"You are a wise man, Caleb MacAfee. I do not fault you for doing what you thought was correct then. Soon Hawk will return to you, and your life will return to normal. This farm is where my brother belongs. He loves the horses as much as he loves his family and Brave Woman. He told me of having a vision of turning the management of this farm to his son as he and Brave Woman grow old together without any of the drama he's been a part of since the beginning of the war."

~ * ~

Although Maude fussed over Soaring Eagle, she wished him well as he began the last leg of his journey. Unlike when he and Matt left with Michael, she insisted on packing food so her son's half-brother would be able to eat without having to hunt for his evening meal. In her heart she thought of him as another of her children and knew she would always hold him in her heart.

She watched as Soaring Eagle packed the food and attached the bundle to the horse he'd chosen as his gift from Caleb. She'd expected he would take a stallion, but instead he chose a chestnut mare. She would, in the future, be the mother to many foals, increasing his herd by good stock.

"I wish I could keep you with us forever," she confessed as he mounted his horse. "I know your place is in your village, but I have enjoyed having you in our home if only for a few hours."

"You are a good woman and have mothered my brother, even though you didn't give him life. In time, I will bring my woman and children to meet you. I know that Summer's Breeze is curious about my brother's white family. When it is possible, I will satisfy her curiosity. I can think of no other white person I would bring her to see. She already knows Brave Woman, Hawk and Caleb. It will be good for her to see a loving woman who isn't afraid to profess her love for someone who is different from her."

With those parting words, he mounted his horse and rode out of their lives as he had ridden into them less than twenty-four hours earlier.

Chapter Seventeen

Matt realized he'd overestimated his ability to make the journey as quickly as he did. He was only in the Shawnee village for two days after Soaring Eagle departed when he developed a fever.

With his body burning, he experienced many visions of the past as well as the future. He saw the massacre of his birth people as though he'd been there, watching the white men who killed men women and children with no thought of the consequences. His vision concentrated on his mother as she gave birth. He could feel the pains of labor that his mother experienced as well as the pressure that pushed him from her womb.

His vision changed to the war he fought, the pain of the musket ball slamming into his shoulder and the worry that he would die before he could get back home, back to Becky.

Visions of the future and the horses he would breed and sell as well as the old age when he and Becky enjoyed their children and grandchildren.

As the fever subsided, so did the visions. He woke to see either the shaman or Rushing Water sitting beside him.

"You had us worried," Rushing Water said when he finally woke up. "You have been unconscious for three days."

"I might have been unconscious in your eyes, but I was experiencing visions of the past and the future. While my brother's future is with the people, mine is on MacAfee farm. It is time for my white father to retire and care for himself. I saw him serving in the government of this new nation and helping shape the world for those yet to come. Without me being able to take over his duties on the farm, this will not come to pass."

"You are a wise man. One who is about to come into his own."

"Have you heard how Michael fares with the Stewarts?"

Rushing Water laughed. "It seems as though the man fears the British as much as he does the Shawnee. I was sent word that he is working well with the horses, and his demeanor has changed dramatically. I doubt you will hear from him again in this lifetime."

"That is good. I feel stronger already."

"Do not push yourself. You are to stay with us until the shaman, and I decided you are well enough to travel the distance between our village and your home. Even then, I will have two braves accompany you so that you do not try to cover too much distance each day."

Matt tried to protest but knew it would do him no good to go against the directive of a chief. He was the guest of Rushing Water. As such, he understood the ability to do as he was told.

"Do you need a maiden to grace your bed?" Rushing water teased.

"You know that is nothing I desire. Becky is far too important to me to betray her trust. We have pledged to each other. Even though we were joined in my father's village, we agreed to wait until we are married in the eyes of the Christian God I grew up worshiping."

"I thought that would be your answer, but I needed to ask out of courtesy to a guest. There are many maidens who would willingly come to your bed. Had Soaring Eagle stayed longer, the same offer would have been made to him."

"My brother's response would have been the same as mine. He is totally devoted to Summer's Breeze and his son. By the time he returns, she should be large with his second child. I know she longs for a daughter, but daughter or son, their child will be raised with love."

~ * ~

Matt remained with Rushing Water and his people for two weeks when the winter snow began to fall. He worried about spending the winter in the village when Rushing Water came to visit him.

"The first dusting of snow has fallen. It won't be long until the heavier snow hits the village. In the morning you and two of my trusted braves will leave for your home to the south."

Knowing the pace Rushing Water insisted he maintain, he would see Becky within a week and insist on having the wedding as soon as possible upon his return. It didn't matter if their home was finished, he didn't want to wait any longer than necessary to make Becky his own in every way that counted.

He was afraid sleep would be a stranger due to his excitement over his upcoming journey. Instead, he fell asleep as soon as he took to his furs.

The next morning, he was up early. As soon as he was finished with the morning meal, he and the two braves who made the journey with Soaring Eagle two weeks earlier, life the village. It was hard saying farewell to Rushing Water and the Shaman, but he promised himself to send back a good breeding mare to increase their herd with an excellent bloodline.

The pace set by his escort was almost annoying. He wanted to let his horse have his head and race across the countryside to get home as soon as possible, but memory of pushing himself to get rid of Michael and the aftermath of it kept him maintaining the more leisurely pace.

Throughout the second day on the trail, a light snow fell. Nothing accumulated, but he knew this was a precursor to the winter about to come.

On the fourth day, he recognized the area. To his right a farm occupied the land which had once held the prosperous village where so many lost their lives during the massacre. He could almost smell the cooking smoke which once dominated the area. By nightfall, he should be home.

Returning to MacAfee farm dominated his thoughts. He longed to see his parents. By morning, he should be ready to go into the village and seeing Becky for the first time in far too long.

~ * ~

"I feel as though our son will be home soon," Caleb said as he and Maude finished their midday meal.

"You've said that every day for the past two weeks. We have no idea what toll the journey north took on him. Winter is about to set in. He could already be snowed in at the Shawnee village. If that is the case, we might not see him until spring when we are ready to take the ship to Scotland."

"You're being too negative. You must have faith that God will bring him back to us soon. Even Becky has stopped coming out here as night falls too early for her to be traversing the distance here. She needs him to be here as much as we do."

Maude agreed with Caleb about how much Becky needed Matt,

but she had doubts about when her youngest son would be returning to the farm soon.

Caleb went out to the stable and Maude busied herself cleaning the kitchen. With everything cleaned to her specifications, she went into the sitting room and picked up her sewing basket. It appears her work was never finished.

It didn't take long until her eyes drooped shut and she fell into a much-needed afternoon nap. For some reason, sleep at night came at a premium these days. It was the same when her boys were off fighting the war. Like a mother hen, she wasn't content when her children weren't near to her.

I'm coming home, Ma, Matt in her dreams said. I've been away far too long. I need to be with my family.

The barking of the dogs woke Maude with a start. She glanced at the grandfather's clock and realized how late she'd slept. She also wondered who would be coming so close to the time for the evening meal.

Getting up she made her way to the porch. To her surprise, she saw Matt dismounting. With him were two braves she didn't recognize. They were not from Soaring Eagle's people as their mode of dress was different.

"Ma," Matt's voice pierced the air. "I can't believe I'm here and you're the first person I've seen." He rushed up the steps and hugged her tightly. "I didn't think I'd ever get back to you. I have so much to tell you about the journey we went on. Where is Pa?"

"I'm right behind you, Son," Caleb said, as he came up to the house from the stable. "I told your mother I was certain you would be home soon and here you are. Have you been to the village to see Becky?"

"Not yet. It's been a long day of traveling. I want to be rested when I see her."

He quickly introduced the braves who came with him and told his father he insisted they come to the farm to get a breeding mare for Rushing Water. "It's the least I can do for the kindness and care he extended to me," he said.

"Will these young men be spending the night?"

"No, they are anxious to use the remaining daylight to begin the return to their families. Once we pick out a mare for them, they will be on their way. They are not as comfortable staying with the whites as Soaring Eagle is."

Maude agreed with her son. Soaring Eagle was comfortable being with them, because of their connection to Matt. They were brothers by blood. Soaring Eagle was comfortable with them because they were Matt's parents by love. To these young braves, they were strangers with a different color skin. In the war, they fought men who looked like them and their apprehension was evident.

While Caleb took the young men to the stable, she hurried into the house to make a nourishing meal for her son. She was thankful for the canned venison she'd put up earlier in the year. It would make for a good supper without the time necessary to cook the meat. To go with the meal, she boiled some new potatoes and freshly dug carrots from her garden. She prayed it would meet with her son's approval.

By the time the potatoes and carrots were cooked to perfection, Caleb and Matt entered the kitchen.

"You didn't have to fuss, Ma," Matt told her.

"I didn't fuss. The girls and I were able to can some venison earlier this year and the vegetables are from my garden. As for the bread, it is some I made this morning. I didn't have time to make a fresh loaf for supper."

"Bread and butter would have been enough for me, but to be truthful, I've had dreams about your cooking."

With grace said and plates full, Caleb asked the question that weighed so heavily on Maude's mind.

"Soaring Eagle stopped here on his way back to the village. He said Rushing Water and Frank Stewart insisted you needed to rest. There must have been more to you being gone so long than that."

"There was. I pushed hard to get rid of Michael. The man was an absolute horror on the trail and did some things I found offensive."

"I know, Soaring Eagle told me of them."

"You didn't tell me," Maude protested.

"It's not something I felt I needed to share with you."

"Since the subject has been broached, I demand to know."

Caleb and Matt exchanged glances telling her they would rather not share the information about Michael.

"Well," she finally said. "Tell me what you know and are keeping from me."

Matt took a deep breath before answering. "On the trail I was ready to ride early in the morning and forced him to get up and prepare to leave. When he said he needed to relieve himself, he exposed himself to me and did as he said he needed to. The man is an obnoxious animal. He didn't have the honor to go into the forest to do his business like anyone else would do. He did it on purpose of course, because he knew it would provoke me to anger. Once we were welcomed into Rushing Water's village, he tried to force himself on one of the women. Only her screams interrupted him and brought help. Had I not promised to take him out of the village the next morning I am certain retribution would have been swift and not at all merciful. He was told if he ever stepped foot within Shawnee territory, he would pay for his deeds."

"You mean they would kill him as they did William," Maude said.

"Yes. The Shawnee, like my father's people, take the forcing of a woman very seriously. It is different for young couples who only couple when the woman is willing. Such things are different among all tribes. Michael fears the Shawnee as well as being turned over to the British in Canada. According to the word we received from Frank, the man has changed and become a good employee."

"That's good but continue about what kept you so long in the Shawnee village," Caleb prompted.

"Two days after Soaring Eagle left to return to his home, I took to my bed of furs. They say I ran a high fever, and they feared for my life. During that time, I experienced visions of the past, the present and the future. I knew I needed to get home, but the shaman and Rushing Water insisted I stay until they deemed me well enough to travel. Had it not been for the men who escorted me, I would have rushed to be here."

"I'm glad you didn't push so hard," Maude said. "I wouldn't want you to have a relapse. There is a young lady in the village who would be disappointed if the wedding had to be postponed any longer than it already has been."

~ * ~

Becky was pleased at how well her employees worked together. When Matt returned to the village, she was more than ready to move to the house she'd been assured was now finished.

Thinking about Matt and his absence from her life brought tears to her eyes that she hadn't shed since he went to war. Already, the winds from the north held a chill and she remembered the snow-covered streets of Philadelphia. She feared he would be forced to spend the winter apart from her.

"I didn't expect to find you crying," she heard someone say from behind her.

She immediately recognized Matt's voice as she turned to face him. "You're here. This isn't a dream. I know I'm awake."

"You are awake and I'm in no way a dream. I've come to claim what is mine. I did stop at the church first. Do you think you can be ready to be married on Saturday?"

"Yes, yes, I can. Do your parents know?"

"I spent the night at the farm. I didn't want to come to you travel worn."

"I would have cared if you came in tatters and tired to the bone, but I understand your need to come to me once you have rested."

"Ma said you haven't been out to the farm since Soaring Eagle was here. I feared you no longer wanted me in your life. Before I came here, I checked the house. It is ready and waiting for us."

"I haven't been out to the farm because you weren't there. I worried you were the one who no longer wanted me. The farm and the house were but a bitter reminder of everything we planned."

"Never for a minute did I think of anything other than making you, my wife. I cursed myself for not consummating out marriage on the night of our joining."

"I have thought the same thing. Thank goodness Saturday is but two days away because I don't think I can wait any longer to be with you."

As though Matt decided he needed to silence her, he kissed her with wild abandonment. It didn't matter if anyone came in and saw them in such an intimate position. She was his and the Indian side of his family dictated his actions.

"Right now, are you Matt or Hawk?" she asked once they broke their embrace.

"I think I'm a combination of both, Hawk has been away for far too long and Matt is here to profess the love he holds for the woman who will soon be his wife in every sense of the word."

"I think I like you best as Hawk. In that persona, you are the most giving and loving man in the world. Just promise me you will never change."

Matt laughed at her statement. "I'm ready to be Hawk only to Soaring Eagle and his people and you. Matt fits better into the white society and as the manager of MacAfee farm, I will be taken seriously with that name."

"No matter what name you use, I am thrilled to think you are mine to love as your father and mother love each other.

~ * ~

The village buzzed with the news of Matt's return and the upcoming wedding. It was a long-awaited event.

With as quickly as things were planned, it was impossible for Richard and Mary to attend the ceremony.

It was Stephen who offered to walk her down the aisle and give her in marriage to Matt. Beatrice volunteered to be her bridesmaid. Things were coming together quickly.

The morning of the wedding dawned with a winter sun and a brisk breeze from the north. Although Becky prepared to wear the dress, she fashioned weeks ago, she wished she was going to be wearing the beautiful white doeskin dress Summer's Breeze loaned her when they were joined in the Indian village.

Susan arrived at the store in time to help her prepare for the wedding. Her nimble fingers fastened the small buttons that lined the back of the dress, then brushed her hair before fashioning it in an elegant style.

"You and Baby Bird make a good couple."

"Lately, Issac, Simon's younger cousin has reopened the forge. Is he someone who could become special for you."

"He has come calling. Ella has been encouraging him to come courting. Everyone seems to approve of him, but I feel we need time to get to know each other better."

"I can understand that. When Matt returned from the war, we needed time to learn who we had become. Neither of us was the same. The war hardened Matt and made me stronger. Since then, we have been through so many trying times, it will be good for the two of us to be settled."

"Do you think you can cope with his weakness?"

"I understand he might also see it as a concern, but we will find a way to overcome it. He has promised me the long life he's seen in his visions. I've learned not to question those visions. Both he and Soaring Eagle experience them. He says it is because his great grandfather was a shaman. Had things been different, that might be the path he sought to also serve the people in that position. Instead, he never had the training. All he has of that part of his life are his visions."

"I'm so glad you have that. I am sorry you have no family to take an interest in the life you are about to embark on."

Becky thought of her family. Her aunt and uncle came to her, only to leave again once the war was over. The only legacy they left her was the knowledge the mansion they stole from Stephen had been turned into a home for the widows in the area. It was true they made things right with Stephen and Beatrice, but they profited greatly from the farms they purchased from the women who were left without husbands to support them.

As for her father, he turned out to be an evil man, who paid for his proposed plans against her and his defiling of the people who gave him refuge with his life. She was relieved to know she never had to worry about him doing her harm again.

Susan finished helping her get ready and left to check on the preparations at the church. She needed to prepare the music for the ceremony.

After one last check in the mirror, Becky was pleased with her appearance. She wanted everything to be perfect for her Hawk.

Stephen waited for her at the base of the stairs, when she heard the bell signal a customer had arrived.

"I'm sorry, we are closed today," she heard Stephen say.

To her surprise the customer was Uncle Richard. "What are you doing here?" she questioned as soon as she saw him.

"It's a long story. From the look of you, I have a feeling I'm interrupting something special."

"Matt and I are getting married this afternoon. I can't believe you have traveled here with the coming winter."

"Winter is why I have come. Your aunt passed away two months ago. It was then I realized there was nothing left for me in Philadelphia. I was able to regain my property, so I sold it and decided to move here. The winters are much milder, and I wanted to be closer to you."

"Where are you staying?"

"As you know, I helped to build a boarding house. I have already settled myself there. I haven't come to take anything away from you. Do you think I will be welcome at your wedding? I realize there were people in this village who were not happy with the way I handled things before Mary, and I returned to Philadelphia."

For a moment, she struggled to come to grips with the reality of Uncle Richard once again living in the village. "Of course, you are welcome at the wedding. I will tell you that Stephen is walking me down the aisle. I need no one to give me away because I was left to my own devices not once, but twice. I am my own woman and run this business better than anyone ever expected. I have even opened a second store."

"Ah yes, the trading posts. I have seen the profits you've received from the trade goods the Indians brought in payment for things they need. I am very proud of you for such venture. The answer to your question is that I did not expect to give you away at your wedding."

"Did you know my father is no longer a threat to me?"

"I have a letter from Stephen detailing with his death. I am sorry you had to be a part of his execution."

"Wasn't a part of it. I refused to watch, as did Matt. It was his father, Caleb, who remained as the witness to his death. I merely stood up to him. He wanted me to defend him. Instead, I told him of the feelings I've kept to myself for years. Of course, that is a story for another day. I am already late for my own wedding. I don't want Matt to think I have left him waiting."

She pushed past her uncle and allowed Stephen to take her arm and escort her across the square to the church where her guests and Matt waited for her.

~ * ~

The closer the time for the wedding became, the more nervous Matt was. With James by his side, he knew he would soon be able to take Becky as his bride. He hoped he would be able to be the husband she deserved.

"You look as nervous as a long-tailed cat in a room full of rocking chairs," James teased. "This is the day the two of you have waited for. Take a deep breath and think about the wedding night."

"You're right. I have no reason to be nervous, but I can't help it. What if she has second thoughts?"

"She's waited this long, I doubt you have any worries about something like that happening."

"I don't know that for certain. It's already half an hour past the time when the ceremony was scheduled to begin. I know that Running Deer is here, and he is uneasy about the delay. So is the shaman."

"How do you know such a thing?"

"You forget my heritage. I have been told in the past my ancestors were shaman. Both Soaring Eagle and I have powers neither of us can explain. Anything is possible and the delay of Becky getting to the church could be proof of her indecision."

He no more than spoke the words, than strains of hymns being played on the piano filled the entire church.

"See, I told you there was nothing to worry about. Susan wouldn't be playing the piano if Becky hadn't arrived. There must be a good excuse for her tardiness."

Matt still had his doubts but put them aside when Thomas opened the door to the sanctuary to lead them to their places at the altar.

Once he stood facing the congregation, he saw farmers, merchants and his two friends from the Indian village sitting side by side. Even though the weather was cool, the women fanned themselves against the heat from the bodies packed together in the church.

In the front row, his parents sat, their smiles putting him at ease. To his surprise in the front pew, on the other side of the church, he recognized Richard Peters sitting next to Stephen's wife and baby.

He wondered how Becky's only relative, a man who returned to Philadelphia over a year earlier, was in the church on this day.

The tone of the music changed as Elizabeth made the walk from the back of the church to stand opposite James. This certainly was turning into a family affair. His brother and sister acting as best man and matron of honor, Susan playing the piano and Ella busy preparing the wedding feast. Along with that Richard Peters sat smiling with pride as if Becky were his child.

Again, there was a change in the music, and everyone got to their feet. Standing in the doorway Becky held onto Stephen's arm, as though she needed the support to walk the short distance to stand by his side.

The beauty of her was accented by the beautiful white satin dress, trimmed in lace that not only fitted her perfectly, but also brought oohs and ahas from everyone gathered to witness the long-awaited wedding. He knew she planned to wear a veil but was not expecting the same lace that trimmed the dress, trimming the crocheted veil.

"Dearly beloved," Thomas said, beginning the ceremony.

He said other words, but Matt didn't hear any of them. He was so taken with the fact he and Becky were going to be joined in marriage, nothing else mattered.

It wasn't until Thomas said, "if there is anyone who has reason why this man and woman should not be joined together, let him speak now or forever hold his peace."

Matt didn't realize he'd been holding his beath until he was certain no one would object to their union.

Vows were exchanged, he in a loud enough voice for everyone to hear, Becky speaking softly, as though the words were for his ears only.

"By the powers vested in me, I now pronounce you husband and wife. What God has put together, let no man put asunder."

With no further prompting, Matt lifted Becky's veil and pulled her into his arms for their first kiss as husband and wife.

"Are we truly married this time?" Becky whispered, once he released her lips.

"We were truly married before, but I couldn't deny you the wedding you deserved, The one sanctioned by the church."

Together they walked, hand and hand to the back of the church, where they would greet their guests.

There were hugs and handshakes from his parents as well as Richard Peters. All the men insisted on kissing the bride for good luck and the women stood on their tip toes to kiss his cheek in congratulations.

The last person to come through the line was a distinguished looking man who was a stranger to Matt. He decided the man had to be someone Becky knew.

"Matt," James said as he stood next to the man. "This is General I mean President Washington. I saw him enter the church close to the end of the service. He would like to meet you."

"On my wedding day?"

"I don't have much time to stay, but I wanted to meet The Savage.

I also would like to have you advise the soldiers who will be serving our new country."

"I'm not a military man," Matt protested. "I'm a farmer with a prosperous farm to manage. It's time for my father to take some time for himself, as he and my mother have a trip to Scotland

planned in the coming weeks."

"So, I've been told. I am prepared to send my key personnel to you. The continuation of MacAfee farm is imperative. So is the information and training you can supply to our troops. I'm talking about two to three weeks a few times through the year. I have no desire to keep you from the duties you have responsibility for."

"I must talk to my wife about this," Matt said. "You are welcome to stay for the feast. My sister has surely prepared far too much food."

President Washington didn't seem to be appalled to think an Indian man called a white man his father and two black women his sisters. It was possible James told him about the make-up of the MacAfee family.

Everyone gathered at Ella's restaurant. As Matt predicted, there was enough food to feed everyone with enough left for Matt and Becky to take out to the farm while they celebrated alone for several days.

For tonight they would stay at the new hotel that had been constructed by a young couple from Boston who wanted to be free of the congestion of the city.

"How long do we have to stay here?" Matt whispered to Becky, as they ate their fill from the food Ella, Elizabth, Susan and Sophie spent days preparing.

"We must cut the cake. Once that is done, your father says he has a surprise for us. I have a feeling he plans on having someone play the bagpipes so we can dance."

Matt smiled, thinking of his father's love for the bagpipes. He'd brought the instrument with him from Scotland and often played it once the evening meal was finished. He had to admit; he liked the sound that came from the odd-looking instrument and looked forward to the nights when his father would play songs he remembered from his childhood.

They had just finished eating when the cake was brought in. There was a large, tiered cake as well as several small side cales. All were frosted in beautiful white frosting decorated with late fall flowers.

As soon as they cut into the cake, Matt realized the top layer was white, while the bottom was a rich spice cake. He was pleased to think his sister made the bottom layer his favorite dessert. He cut a small sliver of cake and fed it to Becky while she did the same for him.

"For my Hawk," she said as she put the cake into his mouth.

Other's must have heard what she said, as many glasses of fine wine and heady ale were raised as the people gathered shouted, "to Hawk and Becky."

Once the crowd quieted, Running Deer added his congratulations. "Among out people, you are known as He Who Stands In Two Worlds. May you and Brave woman live a long and happy life."

His friend's congratulations brought a lump to his throat and tears to Becky's eyes.

The next to stand was the shaman. "The two of you are blessed to be respected in both worlds where you stand. I have a vision of your future, and it is one of prestige, prosperity and happiness. The ancestors speak this truth and on this day your father, Hunting Hawk is smiling with love and pride."

To Matt, those few words solidified the friendship between the people of the two villages. He wished Soaring Eagle was there, but he knew Summer's Breeze was close to the time when she would give birth to her second child. He didn't blame his brother for not wanting to be parted from her.

As he expected, his father left for several minutes and returned wearing a kilt of his family plaid and carrying his bagpipes. Even at his advancing age, Caleb MacAfee was a handsome man, especially when his Scottish heritage was on display for all to see.

Once Caleb began playing the pipes, Matt took Becky in his arms and whirled her around the dance floor. In anticipation of this it was evident his family took the time to teach her the Scottish dances the music demanded be performed.

The people who were assembled either joined them in the dancing or clapped their hands in time to the tune.

"Are you ready to go to the hotel?" he asked, once the obligatory dancing was finished.

"I've been ready for years."

~ * ~

The room at the hotel was no match for the elegant bedroom Becky knew awaited her at their new house. During Matt's absence, Maude had been working decorating the house to meet both her taste as well as those of Matt. Everything was perfect, at least it was to her. Because of being so busy at the store, she'd sent the necessary accessories out to the farm with instructions of how she wanted them to be placed.

On the feather bed of the hotel room lay a beautiful nightgown. As soon as she saw it, her nerves got the better of her. She knew what transpired between a man and a woman, but she didn't know if she was prepared for the pain she knew would come when Matt sacrificed her virginity.

You're a dried up old maid, her father's voice entered her mind. *Only a savage, like Hawk would have the likes of you. Animals aren't partial what bitch they take. Who knows how many other women he's had in the years he was supposedly fighting the war.*

You're wrong. Hawk and I love each other. We have for years, We've been true to each other.

Only her father's bitter laughter continued.

She watched as Hawk took off the clothing he wore. She'd never seen a man without clothing before, and she gasped at the beauty of his smooth body.

"May I have the privilege of helping you out of your wedding dress?" he asked when she hesitated in disrobing.

"I-I would like that," she stammered.

She knew her trembling fingers would not allow her to undo the many fastenings at the back of her dress.

"You're shaking. Are you frightened?"

"A bit. Not of you, but of what is to come during this night of exploration."

"Soaring Eagle tells me the first time there is pain for the woman, but after that, only pleasure. He has instructed me on what to do. Of course, with breeding horses I have an idea of what a man and woman do in their private moments."

"I must know, have you had other women in your bed?"

"How could you ask such a thing? There is no other woman for me other than you. Many times, over the years I was away, women wanted to share my furs. I turned all of them away. I wanted my first time of being a man to be with you,"

Becky breathed a sigh of relief. "I wanted that to be your answer. I've loved you for so long and tonight I plan to give you the most precious gift I have to give."

Chapter Eighteen

Matt awoke with Becky in his arms. *Am I dreaming? Am I really holding the woman I love as I wake from sleep?*

Thoughts of the wedding flooded his mind and brought a smile to his lips.

Beside him, Becky stirred, indicating she was awakening from her first night's sleep as his wife. It was true they'd been married in the Indian village, but at that time he insisted on having a Christian wedding before they consummated their union.

"Good morning, Beautiful," he whispered, as he turned in his arms to face him.

"Good morning, my handsome Hawk, my true and for always husband. Do you want to make love or get dressed for breakfast?"

"Both."

Before he could take her for a morning kiss, there was a pounding on the door.

"Who in the devil would be knocking on our door this early on the morning after our wedding?"

Getting up, he pulled on the britches he'd worn the day before and went to answer the door. To his surprise, James was waiting for him. "President Washington wants to meet with you at ten this morning at the restaurant. I wouldn't want you to be late for such an important meeting."

"What do you know about Washington's plans?"

"More than you think. I traveled with his army during the war. He has approached me to train men to be the first in the field to give medical aid until they can be taken to a doctor. He has always known of your identity as well as your exploits. To say he is impressed with your fighting skills as well as your horsemanship. Aligning yourself with the new government could be very beneficial to your future. He also wants to talk to Father about becoming part of the new government once he returns from Scotland."

"I agree with James," Becky said from beside him.

He turned to look at her and smiled to see she'd wrapped herself in a sheet from their wedding bed.

"I know this isn't what we planned for the morning after our wedding, but we have to think of the future for us as well as for this new country."

"It looks like I'm outnumbered. Give us time to wash up and dress for the morning. We will make the meeting on time."

"We?"

"Becky will be with us as well. She is a shrewd businesswoman. Among the people of my birth, she is known as Brave Woman. In the future, we will need many brave women. It is only proper she be among the first of these women."

"Well said, little brother. I will inform President Washington of your plans. I think he will be receptive to Becky joining us."

James turned to leave. "You are my Brave Woman. Together we will form a fantastic partnership. You have a business background, and I know horses."

"You know so much more than that, my handsome Hawk. You know how to fight for what is right even though your loyalties are in two different worlds. Now, it's time for us to get ready for this meeting with President Washington."

Matt was pleased to think someone brought day clothing to the hotel room. Neatly folded, he found his buckskins along with a clean white shirt. While he dressed, Becky donned a day dress, like the ones she wore when she worked in the store. Seeing her completely dressed, made him wish she was still draped in the sheet she'd worn earlier.

"I love it when you wear your buckskins," Becky said. "You will make a good impression on President Washington, but not unless we leave for the restaurant now."

As much as Matt wanted to stay in the hotel room with Becky, he knew the meeting between them, James and President Washington would be beneficial to their future.

~ * ~

Becky was nervous about the meeting, although she didn't allow it to show. Like Matt said, she knew business, and this was exactly what they would be discussing with President Washington. To her surprise, Caleb was also in attendance.

"Let me begin this discussion," Caleb said, once they were al seated. "Just as the war was a young man's war to fight, the future belongs to the young. I am planning to step back and allow Matt to run MacAfee farm. No one knows the business better than he does. I have never questioned the decisions of my children. Had Matt not returned after the war; I would have had to reevaluate my plans.

"In two weeks, my wife and I will be sailing to Scotland to reunite with my family. We have contacted her family, and they have agreed to meet us in Glasgow. I doubt I would be welcomed in England. Not only because of my Scottish roots but my life in this new country. That said, Matt and Becky will be completely in charge of running the farm.

"When we return, I will consider your offer to become part of your new government, if you are still in need of the opinion of an old Scotsman."

Washington nodded his approval of Caleb's plans. "The army will need highly trained horsemen and good mounts. They have much to learn from the native population about fighting to maintain our independence. The British have retreated to Canada and remain a constant threat. They are busy fighting the French and have enlisted the help of the northern tribes. Whatever promises they have made to these people remain to be disclosed, but whether they keep their word is the unknown.

"In this venture, you will be compensated for your time, as I have some wealthy backers who believe in what I am suggesting to you. We will also need horses and stock from MacAfee farm. It is well known throughout the area and will supply the army with only the best mounts available. This will be a profitable venture for you."

Becky listened to everything that was being said and evaluated their position, should they agree to the proposal.

"What are your thoughts on this, Becky?" Matt asked.

"It sounds like something we want to be part of. From a business point of view, the influx of people coming into the community for training will benefit the restaurant, the hotel, the boarding house, and the store. Our residents will gain and prosper."

President Washington turned his attention to Becky. "It seems you have a head for business, Mrs. MacAfee."

"She should," Caleb said. "She's been running the store by herself since she was fourteen and her father was run out of town. She even opened the trading post to cater to the native population. She has the respect of everyone in this village, as well as the Indian village. I was there when her father was executed for his crimes against Becky as well as the Indians. Becky was given the name of Brave Woman for the way she stood up to the man who was considering unthinkable things against her."

"I saw the Indians at the ceremony. Their respect for these young people was evident. In the future, I will be pleased to have you handling the business part of this proposition."

Becky beamed with pride. Throughout the war she'd heard about General George Washington, now President Washington. He, like Hawk, was her hero. To be in the presence of both men, was an honor that would remain in her memory for the rest of her life.

"My wife makes good sense. It sounds as though we have a deal, Mr. President," Matt said, as he extended his hand to verify his sincerity.

"You are a remarkable young man," President said. "On the battlefield you are The Savage the British called you. In the white world you are a young man who knows what he wants and works to obtain it. From what I hear, no one is better than you with horses. As for your wife, she is a treasure. She knows business and from what I hear has waited a long time to become your wife. If that is not love, then I don't know what is."

Rather than shaking Becky's hand, President Washington took her hand in his and lifted it so he could kiss it.

~ * ~

By evening, Matt and Becky stood in front of the home they'd designed, built and decorated. Instead of walking in side by side, Matt swept her into his arms to carry her over the threshold.

As soon as she was in her arms, she wrapped her arms around his neck. "This was worth the wait," she whispered against his cheek. "We're home, our home. This is where we're raise our children and run the business that I know will prosper and grow."

"I don't care about the business right now. All I want is you and the possibility of creating the children you are hoping for."

Without putting her down, he carried her to the bedroom. The sooner they made love in their new home, the better.

"My, you are anxious. I have a feeling that it is the savage in you coming to the forefront. If so, it can happen for the rest of our lives. I will never tire of seeing Hawk in the bedroom."

~ * ~

Over the next two weeks things moved faster than Becky ever expected them to. While she moved into her new home, Richard decided not to build a house. Instead, he moved into the apartment above the store.

"I think this is the best move. While Stephen is a great manager, I will take over the bookwork. You will still get your portion of the profits. No matter what, you are the owner of this store as well as the trading post. You've earned it through all your hard work. I'm happy to be retired. I plan to teach Stephen how to do the ordering of supplies."

"I-I don't know what to say. I never thought anyone would trust me with owning property. Thank you so much for your confidence in me."

"Confidence, my dear, is earned. I saw potential in you on the day I ordered your father to leave and never return to this area. The fact he couldn't stay away cost him his life. I've spoken with Caleb, and he has told me everything that transpired prior to his death sentence being pronounced. He is lucky I wasn't here when he revealed his evil plans, for I would have delivered a fatal shot to his black heart."

"Did you know where he was during the years he was away from here?"

Becky was surprised at her inquiry. Never had she been interested in where the man was as long as he was no longer in her life.

"The business of running a store is a small community. I heard from a friend in Boston that he had hired a man to work in one of his stores. When he described the man, I knew he was your father. It came of no surprise to hear he'd lost his job for stealing from the store and being abusive to the other employees. He was also loyal to the king, while the man he was working for aligned himself with those who were fighting for the freedom if this country.

"Once he left Boston, it's anyone's guess where he went or how he was able to feed himself. From the condition he was in when he arrived in the Indian village, he was living hand to mouth. It was a far cry from the luxurious life he'd enjoyed once he married my sister."

Becky shook her head, in shame. This was the man who fathered her. From the time of her mother's death, he'd done nothing to nurture her. Instead, he treated her like an unpaid maid. He even made suggestions she should grace his bed so he could use her as though she was his wife. Thank goodness, she'd been able to spurn his advances.

"Are you certain you will be able to manage the stairs to the apartment?" she asked in the attempt to change the subject.

"I'm old, but I'm not fragile. I've already assessed the living conditions of being in the apartment. It will suit me well. I promise, if the stairs become too much, I will make other arrangements. In the meantime, you will not have to worry about the security of the store once it closes for the evening."

"It sounds as though you have everything figured out. If you are comfortable, you are more than welcome to call the apartment home. Will you be hiring someone to cook and clean for you?"

"I've already contacted a man in the village about hiring his daughters to do the work I need done. I've met both girls and they are delightful young ladies. They are adept at cooking and cleaning. Unlike your aunt Mary, I will be paying them handsomely for their service. I am not like your father and have no desire to take either of them to my bed. They are young enough to be my granddaughters. They will get the respect they deserve."

Becky was pleased to see her uncle was no longer the monster who stole property from Stephen and took advantage to Beatrice when she worked for him. He'd returned to being the caring uncle she remembered from her childhood.

~ * ~

The two weeks preceding the sailing of his parents to Scotland passed far too quickly for Matt. Once they left, he and Becky would oversee the farm.

It was James who took them to the dock where his family's ship would sail with his parents on board. As much as he didn't want to see them leave, he was pleased they were returning to see the family they left behind so many years earlier.

"We will be back in the fall," his father assured him. "By that time, I'm certain we will be ready to return to our American family. As my father used to say, after four days fish and house guests begin to stink. We will be extending that time and seeing everyone we want to see and be ready to come home."

Chapter Nineteen

Caleb and Maude stood on the deck as the shoreline of Scotland came into view. "This is my home," he said. "Are you ready to meet my family?"

"After meeting Michael, I am worried about what they will think of me. I'm not Scottish. What if they hate me?"

"How could anyone hate you?"

"I'm English, isn't that enough?"

"I don't see you as a threat. It seems to me I fell in love with you at first sight. They will too."

Together, they stayed on deck until the ship docked in Aberdeen Harbor. To calm Maude's nerves, Caleb pulled her into a tight embrace, kissing away her fears.

When they finally docked and disembarked, Caleb searched the crowd for his brother Sean. He was easy to spot, and it was like looking into a mirror of what he would look like in the future.

"Caleb, over here," Sean called.

Taking Maude's hand, he hurried them through the crowd to get to the brother he hadn't seen in far too long. "Sean, it's good to be home and to see you. Will we be able to get to your farm before dark?"

"I'm afraid it's too long a trip to make before dark. I have arranged rooms for us at the inn. Now, introduce me to this bonnie lass. She is a beauty. It's no wonder you fell in love with her when you first met."

"Sean, this is my wife, Maude. She's a bit worried about meeting all of you."

"There's nothing to worry about Maude," Sean assured her. "We're family. I know your heritage, but since my brother loves you, who am I to hold your heritage against you? Caleb has never made it a secret. I know you are planning to meet with your family in Glasgow, but I took the liberty of inviting them to the farm. They should arrive there tomorrow."

"I can't believe you would do this for us," Maude said, speaking for the first time. "Are you certain my family won't be imposing?"

"Positive. We have just built a house for our grandson, who is getting married just before you are scheduled to leave. It will be perfect for your family to stay there. My grandson, Aaron, is excited to meet everyone and had no problem with them staying in the house he will occupy with his wife.

"Speaking of children, what do you hear of Michael? You letter said you kicked him out of your home when he became overbearing."

"Our son, Matt, took him to the Stewart farm to the north of us. They knew what they were getting into, because Maude contacted them to see if they would accept Michael. One their way to the farm, Matt and his brother Soaring Eagle stopped with Michael in the village of the Senica. While they were there, Michael tried to force one of their women. He was banned from their village. By working at the Stewart farm, I think good things will come for him. They won't allow him to peruse his old ways. Should he leave via the territory of Senica, he is under a mandatory death sentence. If he were to go north, he would run into the British in Canada. He has no choice but to change his ways and become a productive person."

"It's hard to believe. I couldn't tolerate his whoring, drinking and gambling. I'm pleased to know he has possibly found a place where he can begin a new life. Enough of this talk. I will leave you to the nighttime pleasures of a man and his wife. Hopefully you will get some sleep, because we need to make an early start tomorrow morning. I am anxious to get home, and the family is anxious to finally meet you, other than through the letters you send. Also, Maude's family should be arriving soon. I am certain they are as anxious for this reunion as we are."

Caleb was as overwhelmed by Sean's generous offer as Maude. When he planned this reunion of the two families, he never expected his brother would take things a step further and mesh the families together.

After partaking of a meal at the inn, Caleb and Maude went to their upstairs room. "I feel like a young bride again," Maude confessed, as Calab fitted the key into the lock.

"This is our first night has husband and wife on Scottish soil. If I were younger and stronger, I would carry you across the threshold like I did when we first moved into our house."

"I'm afraid if you tried something like that tonight, you might put out your back. I have better plans for our first night on Scottish soil and they don't include you being in pain. The only pain I want you to experience is that of your desire for me. You've always been a fantastic lover. I doubt tonight will leave either of us wanting."

~ * ~

As soon as they finished eating breakfast, they got into Sean's coach for the trip to the farm. The closer they got to their destination, the more concerned Maude became.

Her family didn't approve of her first husband, James' father. When they got married because she was pregnant with James, they disowned her. Since she moved to the new world, she'd received sterile letters each year at Christmas. It was hard to imagine they were excited about this reunion.

The coach drove through the Scottish countryside. Even though the scenery was breathtaking, Maude was fixated on what she would find at the end of her journey.

While Sean readily accepted her, how would her brother, George, react to seeing her again after so many years? He did write and tell her of the passing of their parents, but never once did he suggest they somehow reconnect.

The house at MacAfee farm resembled the one Caleb built for her, settling her nerves slightly. Standing on the porch, was a man who could have been her father. Knowing he was already dead and buried for many long years, she knew the man had to be her brother.

"Maude? Is it true? Are we finally meeting after all these years?"

George hurried to the carriage to help her alight before Caleb could do the honors.

"Thank God for Sean MacAfee for finding us. He sent his own coaches to bring us here for this long overdue reunion."

"I didn't think you would want anything to do with me. Had I not married James' father, he would have been labeled a bastard."

"That was Father who held those feelings. By the time of his passing, he'd instilled the same feelings within the rest of us. The distance between us and you only allowed us to carry on the old hurts. It was Sean who told us of the life you have led since you, and Caleb were married. He told us that you are well respected in your area. Also, of the children you have birthed as well as the ones you have taken into your home when they had no other place to go. I even learned about the involvement of family during the war. To be truthful, I hold no love for our king. If I wasn't so well established in England, I would consider moving to the new world just to be rid of him."

"You certainly know more about my life than I know of yours. You said Sean brought the entire family here. What of my sister, Bernadine?"

"Unfortunately, she passed in her sleep just three weeks ago. She was looking forward to meeting you. Her daughter, Anne, is here as a representative of her branch of the family. Our sister Claudia is also here. Although she was but a mere child when you left home, she has heard all the stories Bernadine told her to keep you alive in her mind. She is as excited as I am for this time we will have together. I can't begin to thank Sean enough for orchestrating this."

All the butterflies that had taken flight in her belly over this reunion suddenly disappeared. Her family did want her. She was not the outcast her father disowned so many years earlier.

~ * ~

Sean's house was filled with members of his family as well as those who came from England to meet with Maude. When they entered the main hall, all conversation ceased.

Sean's children and grandchildren, who had been little more than names in his brother's letters, greeted them warmly.

"Did you fight the Indians?" Sean's youngest son, Patrick asked.

"There was no need for a fight. The tribe living close to our farm is friendly. You must know my youngest, Matt, is of their people."

"You called him Matt, I thought he went by the name Hawk," Sean commented.

"As a child, he wanted to honor his Indian father, Hunting Hawk," Maude explained. "We have always remained close to the man who fathered him. When the war broke out, he decided to fight in his own way. He and the braves from his father's village fought many battles. To the British, he was The Savage. As a child it was a name he hated. As an adult, he embraced it, knowing he fought valiantly for the independence of our new country. When he returned home, he took back his Christian name. Of all our children, he is the one who will continue running the farm."

"What of James?" George asked.

"He wanted to be of service to others. Although he loves our farm and horses, he loves medicine more. He and his wife, Sophie, have prospering practice and are coming to think of bringing in a second doctor. He also followed President Washington as a camp doctor during the war. Just recently, he has been visited by President Washington to see if he would be willing to train young men to serve in the army and treat the wounded before they are transferred to field hospitals.

"Matt has also been contacted to train men to become proficient horsemen and fighters. It's a great honor. I have been contacted as well to serve in the government. I am still contemplating my answer."

"If Matt is working for the president, who will be managing the farm?" Sean asked.

"Matt will continue to manage things for us, as the men he will be training will be coming to the farm. When I left, a new building was being constructed for these men to stay during their training. It wouldn't surprise me if the Indian village is moved closer to the farm so the men who fought with Matt can assist him with the training."

"You speak of these Indians as though you know them," George pressed.

"I do know them. It was in their village that Matt first married Becky. The Indians call them Hawk and Brave Woman. The chief, Running Deer, and the shaman were at the church wedding. To them, Matt is one of their own."

"If they were already married," Aaron began, "why would there be a church wedding?"

"At the time of the ceremony in the Indian village, Becky didn't want to be separated from Matt. Together, they decided- not to consummate their union until after the church service. Of course, the timeline for the ceremony was altered because of having to escort Michael to the Stewart farm. They are now married in ways that honor both of his heritages. When we left, they were happier than I have ever seen either of them. They were meant to be together from the first moment they met. Of course, at the time, they were children. They would have been married sooner, had the war interfered. It's no wonder that Matt wanted everything to be perfect on the day they were joined together by a minister, in the eyes of God."

"I'm certain there are many more stories to be told," Sean's wife, Judith, said. "For now, our meal is ready. I didn't hire two young women from the village to prepare food that is going to get cold. We have to months to learn everything our brother must tell us."

Chapter Nineteen

Matt was well-satisfied with the way his life was turning out. He and Becky approached Running Deer about the proposition President Washington gave him.

Running Deer looked at Matt with a wide grin on his face. "You know I have considered you as another son. I think we can be of help to you with the training. I have been talking with the shaman, and he told me of a vision he experienced after your wedding. In it, he saw us moving our village closer to your farm so we can be of help in training the soldiers who will be coming to learn of our ways of fighting."

"I too had a vision, not unlike the one the shaman experienced. I would like nothing more than to have the people of my birth closer to me. I'm certain Becky would not object to moving the trading post closer to the new village."

"This will not happen in the blink of an eye, but it will happen before the winds of winter blow across the area."

The meeting ended and Matt said goodbye to his Indian friends.

He found Becky in he apartment, packing the last of her belongings for the move out to the farm.

"Did you talk to Running Deer before he left?"

"I did and he is considering moving the village closer to the farm. That just leaves the trading post. It is no situated close to the village, but if they move…"

"I see no problem in relocating the trading post," Becky said, silencing him with her finger to his lips. "It was established to service the Indian village. Should they move, there is no reason for it to continue in its current position. Moving and building a bigger and better trading post will service not only the Indians but also the settlers in the area."

Rather than continuing their conversation, Matt kissed Becky, leading her to bed. Suddenly, he was planning on tossing her skirt, as his father would say, and making love to her in the bed she'd shared with no one else. It was only right that they use it at least once.

~ * ~

Becky loved her new home. It did seem odd not to have to go to work at the store each morning, but at the same time, she knew this was the life she'd wanted ever since she was a little girl.

With Matt's parents on their way to Scotland, she understood the extra work needed to be done by her husband. She didn't mind, because he seemed happiest when he was with his horses. He praised the new colts and looked forward to the day when he would be receiving buyers from all over the new country.

Even with the older generation away for an extended period, the main house brimmed with activity. Susan still lived at home. She came to visit daily to see if they needed anything from the village.

Becky loved Susan's visits, as she had become her best friend. Being the same age, it was like having a sister she always longed to have.

"So how is Baby Bird handling everything?" she asked over coffee and the scones Maude taught her to make.

"I can't believe you still call him that," Becky teased. "To answer your question, he is in his glory. Each morning, he is anxious to get out to the stable and when we are together, he regales me with stories of whichever horse he has been working with. I think he's a bit worried that we haven't had any buyers, but it will take time for them to adjust to him running the farm and not Caleb. It's still early in the season. Although it is spring here, I remember these months from when I lived in Philadelphia. It was not unheard of for there to be snow in April and early May. If the weather is not cooperating it will take longer for them to be willing to travel."

"It pleases me he is doing something he loves so much. I worry about this proposal from President Washington. I know James is excited about the possibility of being part of the new government, but will it be too much for Baby Bird?"

Again, Becky cringed at the nickname Susan insisted on using. "Matt is looking forward to the opportunity. He has even spoken to the Indians, and they are considering moving their village closer to the farm so they can be of help with this training."

Susan finished her scone and coffee before leaving for the village.

Her position at the restaurant was as Matt's managing the farm.

Becky lingered over her second cup of coffee, contemplating everything they talked about. She knew she should be preparing their dinner, but became so lost in her thoughts, she didn't realize the amount of time that passed.

"I need to go into the village and pick up the mail," Matt said, interrupting he inner musings. "I thought you might like to check on the store and eat dinner at the restaurant. I can feel hunger pains gnawing at my stomach and I don't smell anything cooking in the kitchen."

"I'm sorry, as thinking about the future. Susan brought up some interesting things."

"I know what she said. She's worried about me not being able to handle the training of the soldiers along with managing the farm. Do not let it weigh too heavily on your mind. I have good men to do the work I merely oversee. I get to reap the pleasure of working with the horses, while they do the work. As for the training, Spotted Pony was at the stable this morning and the elders have voted to move the village closer to the farm. I will have the best of both worlds. My parents will return from Scotland to help me and my brother as well as his people will be close enough for them to get to know my children."

He placed his hand on her flat stomach. "Do you carry my child?"

"If I don't it's not because we haven't been trying. Yes, I do think we have made a baby. Only time will tell for sure."

"Even if you just think you are pregnant, you should visit James' office while we are in the village. I want you to have the best care possible. This child, as well as its mother, are the most important people in my world. It's too bad we don't have time to make love before we leave for the village. I never tire of showing you how much you mean to me."

"You are incorrigible. I swear, if you had your way I would never leave our bed. Of course, if that were the case, I wouldn't be able to cook your meals, and you would starve."

It came as no surprise to see the carriage hitched to a horse and waiting for them. As they started toward the village, a light breeze blew, ruffling her hair and causing her to put her shawl closer around her shoulders.

"It's a perfect day for a ride through the countryside. Is there anything you need to purchase at the store? Perhaps we should look for a cradle."

"I'm not even sure if I am pregnant."

"If not now, soon. Father says Mother was pregnant with Elizabeth shortly after they arrived at the farm. At that time, they were living in a tent, much like I liked to do when I was younger."

"I hope you don't expect me to sleep in your tent."

"It is an intriguing idea," he said, giving her a sly wink. "Who knows, you might like sleeping on the furs."

"I did that in the Indian village and to be truthful, it wasn't the best sleep I've had in my life."

"The difference is that in my tent we would be making love. I would find that most enjoyable. We have the rest of our lives to decide when the time might be right for us to consider such an adventure."

The buildings of the village came into view, ending their playful conversation. Everywhere people were busy building new structures and going about their daily routine.

Their first stop was at the restaurant. "You left my bride with much to think about," he greeted Susan. "Unfortunately, she was so busy thinking, she was unable to prepare our dinner. I hope you and Ella have something special on the menu today."

"We always have something special. Today, it is a hot roast beef sandwich with beef gravy and mashed potatoes. Ella has also used some of the cherries we canned last year to make cherry pies. Is that enough to whet your appetite?"

"More than enough. Do you have cold milk and hot coffee."

"You know we do."

"Good, then we will each have a cup of both."

"While they waited for their meal to be served Maude reached her hand across the table to intertwine her fingers with those of her husband. "I like it when you order for me. I normally don't order milk."

"You aren't normally carrying my child. If you are pregnant, the milk is good for you as well as the baby."

"What if I'm not pregnant?"

"Even so, the milk won't hurt you. When I was fighting the war, I found it was the one thing I missed the most, other than you. Ma always served milk with our meals. It's something I never expected to miss as much as I did."

With their dinner finished, Ella came into the dining area of the restaurant. "Susan told me you were here. I have the children put a basket of food in your carriage. That way you won't have to prepare supper when you get home. I know how a trip to the village can tire you when you are in such a delicate condition."

"How did you know? I'm not even sure."

"Susan is very good at detecting these things. She said she had her suspicions this morning. She could see it in your eyes. I never question her ability. My mother, back in Africa, was considered a seer, one who can see into the future and read people's feelings by looking into their eyes. Unfortunately, I did not retain such a gift."

"I've got to stop associating with people who can see into the future," Becky teased, as she winked at Matt. "It's bad enough that my Hawk can see into the future. Now you tell me Susan can do the same thing. Combine that with the shaman from the Indian village and Soaring Eagle, I'm never going to be able to keep a secret."

"I hope you have no secrets to keep from me," Matt replied. "I want no secrets between either of us for the rest of our lives."

~ * ~

A stop at James' office confirmed the assumptions she'd had for the past few days. If Becky's calculations were correct, she'd conceived on their wedding night, meaning within the next seven months they would welcome their new baby.

With the knowledge of their baby, she made her way to the store. To her surprise, Richard was greeting customers.

"I didn't think you wanted to work in the store," she greeted him.

"I'm not working, I'm socializing. It gets lonely sitting in the apartment working on the books all day. I've met the most interesting widow woman. Her name is Isabelle and she's close to my age. We've become great friends and have some of the same interests. She's been teaching me to play cribbage. It seems her husband was a woodworker and made cribbage boards as gifts. I do find the game to be not only interesting, but it strengthens my skills in mathematics."

Becky smiled. She'd not heard of the game before but decided to invite Richard and his new friend out to the farm for Sunday dinner. It was possible they might be able to teach them how to play cribbage.

It might be a pleasant way for her and Hawk to spend an enjoyable weekend as they awaited the birth of their first child.

"As long as you're happy, I think your new friendship is a good thing. Perhaps you and Isabelle would like to come out to the farm on Sunday for dinner and teach us this new game you are so fond of playing."

"I'll have to ask her. I think we should be able to make it. Let the meal be our treat to you. Isabelle makes a baked ham that brings tears to your eyes it is so good."

"We'd be honored," Matt said, joining the conversation. "As for cribbage, perhaps I can show you, my expertise. It is used to be one of my mother's favorite games to play with us. She said she thought it was something we should learn, to sharpen our mathematics skills. I doubt I would be able to do math in my head if it hadn't been for that game."

"I didn't know you knew how to play cribbage," Becky said. "I feel like I'm the only one who wasn't taught such a game."

"You hardly had time for games when you were growing up, my love. It seems to me you were busy with the store and making the apartment your home. We can start your lessons in the game tonight, since we don't have to worry about preparing supper. I don't think playing cards is appropriate for a Sunday afternoon. Why don't we plan for Saturday. I don't think the good Lord would object to card playing on a day other than the sabbath."

Everyone laughed at Matt's comment. Becky tended to admit how sacred her husband held the teachings of the church. Even though he practiced ways of his birth people when he was with them the Christian God meant more to him than anything else.

Chapter Twenty

The remainder of the summer passed in almost a blur for Matt. The entire village of his birth people as well as the trading post moved closer to the farm. The warriors who fought with him during the war were close at hand when the men Washington chose to send to the farm for training arrived. While he trained the men in horsemanship teaching them to ride and be able to shoot at a target at the same time, the warriors, imparted their knowledge of ground fighting.

As Becky promised him, the height of summer brought the horse buyers. They came from all over the colonies, now called states.

"I worried about Caleb not being here," one of the buyers said as he and Matt made a deal for three riding horses. "I'm of a generation that thinks the younger men aren't as well trained as their fathers. In your case I must apologize for my assumptions. You are as adept as your father. I've been told you are the one the British called The Savage. I thank you for your service throughout the war that won our freedom."

"I take your words as a high compliment. The horses I have for sale are the best MacAfee farm can produce. I was taught well."

"Where is Caleb?"

"My parents left this spring for two months in Scotland to reconnect with their families. I have had one letter saying that the voyage over was smooth and they were looking forward to the reunion."

"When he returns, I will send him a letter and let him know he has left his holdings in good hands."

Other buyers came and voiced the same opinions. None of them questioned why an Indian man was carrying the MacAfee name or was in control of the farm including the sale of the horses they bred with great pride. They had been doing business with his father for years and knew the stories behind the strangely mixed family.

~ * ~

As the summer proceeded, the small bump protruding from Becky's body, told him their child was growing.

"Do you want a son or a daughter?" Becky asked, as they ate supper one evening.

"I'm torn. Of course I would like a son, what man doesn't, but the thoughts of a daughter who resembles her beautiful mother keep crowding into my mind. I keep hoping for a premonition about the sex of the baby, but I haven't had any visions to reveal such personal information."

"That's good, because I want us both to be surprised at the birth. I, too, am confused as to what I want. Being an only child, I had no siblings, male or female. I would love a little boy who looks like you, but a little girl would be just as welcome. More than anything else, I would like to have a healthy baby. Boy or girl, it doesn't matter. Whichever, it was conceived in love and will be raised in love as well. In this crazy family, any and every child is welcomed."

Becky prayed nothing would go wrong before the child could be born. She'd heard too many horror stories about women miscarrying their first child and being unable to conceive again.

As she did often, she put her hand over her expanding midsection. When she did, she felt a flutter, not unlike a butterfly ripple across her belly.

"I think our child has been listening to our conversation," she said.

"What are you talking about?"

"The baby moved for the first time. It's been four months since we conceived. It's time for the movement to begin. At least that's what James told me at church on Sunday. Feeling the movement makes it seem real. Before it was but a glorious dream."

"I like your glorious dream and can hardly wait until I can feel our child for myself. I doubt I would be able to feel a butterfly, but the movement will become more active in the future, and I will be about to feel a bit of what you do."

~ * ~

"As much as I want to stay here in Scotland, I am anxious to return home," Caleb said, as he and Sean watched the training of the young horses.

"At our age, this will probably be the last time we meet in this lifetime. To say I'm looking forward to you returning to America would be a lie. I would enjoy having you closer than an ocean away from me. I do understand your need to return home. We have had a good visit, and you've got to know my family. When did you say you sail?"

"The ship leaves in a week from today. What's to say you and your wife, Judith, couldn't accompany us and spend the winter on the farm?"

"We'd have to talk about it. It's not as though I'm needing to manage the farm. As you have seen, I do little of the work, leaving that to the younger generation."

"I was hoping you would agree with me. Tonight, we will speak with the wives and see what they have to say on the subject."

As much as Caleb wanted to broach the subject of his brother and sister-in-law coming to America, he held his tongue until they were enjoying an evening brandy in the library. The women both sipped on glasses of fine wine.

"Maude and I have been talking," Judith said before either of the men could utter a word. "What is there to keep us here on the farm? Maude has invited us to spend the winter on their farm. At first, I didn't know how to reply, but I have always wanted to travel."

Her statement brought laughter from Sean.

"What is so funny about what I just said?"

"Nothing, my love. It's just that Caleb and I were talking this afternoon and decided to broach the subject of us going to America with them. We were worried that it would take hours of talking to convince you to take such a journey."

"We were worried about you opposing the idea," Maude said. "I guess what they say is true, great minds do travel on the same road."

The remainder of the evening was spent making the plans necessary for the trip. Caleb and Sean would have to go to Aberdeen and book passage for two more people on the voyage. While they did that, Maude and Judith would be busy with packing the clothes necessary for the prolonged stay.

"What do you think the children will say?" Judith asked, as the lists of duties were made.

"They'll be happy for us. In case you haven't been listening, Edward has been urging us to go to America for a visit ever since the end of the war. Aaron is settled with his new bride and neither of them need the older generation looking over their shoulders. Added to that is the fact I would like to see Caleb's operation and meet his family."

"Don't forget the horses you sold to me. I can use all the help I can get to see to them throughout the voyage. I find the sea air makes me fall in love with my wife again. We plan to spend much of the trip in our cabin making love."

"Caleb, how can you talk about such personal things?" Maude asked.

"I only speak the truth. As you recall we enjoyed some good times in our bunk when we were coming here. I'm looking forward to doing so again."

He loved to watch Maude's face turn from her normal coloring to almost a bright red in embarrassment. It wasn't like he was making things up. Even after all these years together, they enjoyed a healthy love life.

~ * ~

"I've received a letter from Pa," James said when they met in church on Sunday morning. His ship will be arriving on Wednesday and he's bringing guests with him."

"Guests?" Matt questioned. "The last time we had a guest from Scotland, it was Michael. I hope he's not planning to bring home another misfit."

"Hardly. It seems he has persuaded Uncle Sean and Aunt Judith to spend the winter at the farm. Who knows, he might even take a trip up to the Stewart farm to visit Michael."

"I don't mind having the company, but they might not be going to the Stewart farm. I had a letter from Ma's friend, and she said Michael left. He said he wanted to go out to the west where he wouldn't have to contend with the constraints of living by someone else's rules. He'll be lucky if he is able to survive on his wits alone. From what I've heard, there are some warring tribes that he might run into."

"That's a shame. After the first letter you received, I had great hope the man was turning his life around."

Matt crossed the church to where Becky and several of the women were engaged in conversation. Among the group was Richard's friend, Isabelle.

"I was telling Becky that I have been making some baby clothes for her," Isabelle said. "I know she is busy with running a home and carrying a baby. It can be quite tiring. Many of the other women are making blankets and clothing as well. Anything to take some of the more tedious tasks from her shoulders."

The generosity of the people in the village never ceased to amaze Matt. It was as though the war helped them to form a bond with each other.

"Are you ready to go home?" Matt asked Becky.

"I must admit I am. Even the short journey into town and the church service have made me quite tired."

They said goodbye and headed out for their carriage. If this short trip tired her out, how would she handle guests for the entire winter?

"We have something to talk about," Matt began as they drove out of the churchyard. "Ma and Pa will be home a week from Wednesday."

"That is wonderful news. I've missed them terribly."

"They are bringing Uncle Sean and Aunt Judith with them. They plan to spend the winter at the farm, since a winter voyage can be difficult, or so Pa says."

"I know your father misses his family. It is good that they have found a way to extend their relationship. If you're concerned about me overdoing things while they are here, I doubt that will happen. They will all be staying at the big house and will probably be over to see if they can help every day. I don't think I will turn down their help. It should prove to be an interesting winter, to say the very least."

~ * ~

The following Saturday, the entire family came out to the farm to begin cleaning and dusting in preparation for Caleb and Maude's return.

"We certainly don't want Ma to come home to a dusty house," Elizabeth said, as she polished the dining room table and the sideboard with lemon oil.

"I'll come back on Wednesday and give the house a once over while James is picking everyone up at the docks," Sophie added.

"That won't be necessary," Becky protested. "I'm more than capable of doing that much. So far, none of you have allowed me to do a thing."

"Doctor's orders," James said from behind her. "I saw how tired you were at church on Sunday. I don't want you to overexert yourself. This baby is too important to my brother as well as the family to risk you becoming too tired."

"I'm not an invalid, but I will follow your instructions. Even Soaring Eagle has sent Summer's Breeze here to help whenever she can. Although I do enjoy playing with their children, I worry that everyone is being overly cautious."

"Of course we are cautious. You are very important to our family. Not only are you my brother's wife, but you have been an unofficial family member ever since you first arrived. It was especially so when your father was asked to leave the settlement and never return. You don't know how proud everyone in the village is of how you have handled running the store on your own."

Becky blushed at the compliment. For years she thought she was alone in the world when from the very beginning of she had the support of everyone she knew.

~ * ~

As the ship finished the docking procedures, Caleb scanned the faces of the people waiting to greet the passengers who made the long voyage from Scotland, England and Ireland to America. He smiled when he recognized his sons standing on the dock watching the ship complete its journey.

It was amazing how alike and yet how different they were. James was the picture of what one would think of a doctor. He was dressed in the latest fashion and had a stance of a man of importance. On the other hand, Matt was dressed in his buckskins, along with fringe moccasins. Like his brother, Matt carried an air of self-confidence. Both wore their hair long, James' hair was drawn back into a que at the back of his head, held with a satin ribbon, while Matt's hair was perfectly braided in a style that reminded Caleb of the men in the Indian village.

"Are those your sons?" Sean asked, as he followed Caleb's stare.

"Yes. I didn't expect Matt to come. I thought for certain he would send one of the stable boys. I did know James would be here, because this is the day the office is closed."

"I'm afraid I'm going to have a hard time calling your youngest son Matt. To me he has always been Hawk and to look at him, the name fits him perfectly. Since you knew his Indian father, do you see a resemblance?"

"I do. I see it in his brother, Soaring Eagle, as well. They make a striking pair when the two of them are together. Now that the Indian village has moved closer to the farm, we will be seeing much more of him as well as the others I've gotten to know. They are good people. It is a shame there are men who look down on them because they live as their ancestors did. They are a noble race of people and deserve more respect than many of our race have given them."

The ship finished docking. Once it was time to leave and step on firm ground, Sean sought out Judith, while Caleb did the same. With Maude on his arm, he led the way to the gangplank.

"Pa, it's so good to see you and Ma," Matt said, rushing toward them.

"It looks as though the summer away from the farm did you a world of good," James added, as he pumped his father's hand and hugged his mother tightly.

"Boys, this is your Uncle Sean and Aunt Judith. I hope my letter reached you saying they will be spending the winter with us."

"Of course it did," James replied. "The girls have been busy getting the house cleaned and ready for the four of you to arrive. Ella even sent Susan out to the farm to prepare the evening meal for you."

Caleb noticed a look of concern on Matt's face. "What of Becky?"

"James has left strict orders for her to rest. She is expecting and we are all concerned about the fact she tires so easily."

"It doesn't surprise me," Maude said. "She has had years of running the store. Even though she isn't there every day, she still worries about how things are going. Added to that, she has not had the time to rest that most young ladies enjoy. Pregnancy, under the best of circumstances, is tiring. It is good she has James to oversee her care and make certain we are gifted with a healthy grandchild."

As the cargo was unloaded, Caleeb and Sean picked out their traveling trunks and retrieved the four horses Caleb purchased to enhance their stock. While Sean protested about taking any money, they concluded that Caleb would buy one mare and a stud while Sean gave him the other two mares.

"I hope those horses are coming to the farm," Matt said, his voice filled with awe and the prime lines of the horses.

"Yes, they are. They come from Sean's stable and will be an added addition to the herd we already have."

Matt was quick to hurry over to take the reins of the four horses and tie them to the back of the wagon he brought to transport the baggage to the farm, while James drove the coach.

"Did you see the light in your son's eyes when he saw the horses?" Sean asked. "It is evident he shares our love of good horseflesh."

"Even as a child, Matt preferred the company of the horses to anything else. Many years ago, I traded horses with Matt's birth people. They are expert horsemen and taught Matt much more than I could ever hope to know. He rides like an Indian. He's as comfortable riding bareback as he is with the saddle. President Washington made a good choice when he asked Matt to train his soldiers."

"We have everything loaded into the wagon," Matt said, once the horses were securely tied to the back of the wagon. James will be bringing around the coach soon and we can be on our way."

"If your father doesn't mind," Sean replied, "I would like to ride with you in the wagon. Looking at the seat, there is room for two maybe even three people."

"I would be honored, but the coach would be far more comfortable for the trip back to the farm."

"I agree with your uncle," Caleb said. "If I'm not mistaken, your sister sent a lunch. We will take our portion of the food and both ride with you. I'm certain the ladies would be happier without us hovering over them. If we're lucky there might be a couple of bottles of wine for us to share."

"You know us too well, Pa. Ella came out to the farm this morning, before she opened the restaurant and left off the food backet, along with the twins. They are so anxious to see their grandfather. Of course,

Sophie and Elizabeth are both at the house with their children. It might be good if Ma and Aunt Judith get a short nap before they arrive to the chaos of your grandchildren."

~ * ~

Matt enjoyed the company of his father and uncle on the trip to the farm. As he predicted, grandchildren played on the lawn and squealed with delight when he pulled into the dooryard.

His father's feet no more than hit the ground than he was surrounded by grandchildren, all vying for his attention. He was soon down on one knee delighting in the attention of the children.

"I swear you've all grown several inches while your grandmother and I were gone."

"Where is Grandma?" James' oldest, Hattie, asked.

"She is with your father in the coach. She's with your Aunt Judith, so he took things a little slower than we did. They should be here any minute."

"Are you our Uncle Sean?" Hiram asked.

"That I am, lad. It will take me a while to learn all your names. We will have all winter to become acquainted."

"Do you have grandchildren, Uncle Sean?"

"Not as many as my brother, but yes, I do. They are much older though. They are closer to Matt's age than to you."

The arrival of the coach ended the childish questions as all attention was focused on the occupants of the closed vehicle.

"Grandma," the children called, as though they practiced saying the word together.

Matt smiled. Soon, his son or daughter would be among the children giving their grandparents such joy.

"I missed all of you dearly, but I have wonderful stories to tell you of our visit to Scotland and everything we did and saw while we were there."

Surrounded by the children, the four members of the older generation made their way to the house. Matt hung back. He knew he would find Becky resting in the house, but that rest would be interrupted with the arrival of rest of their family.

"Aren't you coming in?" Becky inquired.

He looked up to see her standing on the porch, her hands on her hips. "I was just taking everything in. I didn't know if you would be at the main house or resting at our home."

"I wouldn't miss out on this reunion for anything in the world. I have been resting all day in anticipation of seeing your parents again. For now, the children hold their attention. Once everyone returns to their homes we will have our private time with them."

"Pa and Uncle Sean insisted on riding with me in the wagon. We had a good conversation, but for now, I must see to the new horses Pa brought with them from Scotland."

"From the looks of things, John and one of the stableboys have everything under control with the horses. You will have plenty of time to work with them in the coming days."

Matt looked over his shoulder to see John tenderly stroking the noses of the new stock. He knew the stock was in good hands, even though he longed to be with them and make certain they were properly cared for. Instead, he followed Becky into the house and the chaos surrounding the arrival of his parents along with his aunt and uncle.

~ * ~

One by one the families returned to their homes, leaving the older adults to enjoy glasses of after dinner brandy and wine.

"That's quite the brood you have," Sean teased. "I never expected such a warm welcome."

"We are a close family. It matters not whether our skin is white, black or copper, we love each other and are blind to the differences. If we would have had the chance to bring more children into our lives, we wouldn't have hesitated, no matter what their race might be."

"You are, most definitely a caring man. Everyone in your family is blessed to have been brought into your household. I have never been as proud of anyone as I am to be able to call you brother."

Chapter Twenty-One

Matt was thrilled to have Sean helping him with the horses. He learned things he never knew existed. New techniques that not only enhanced the training process but seemed to put the horses more at ease.

Little by little the warmth of summer gave way to the chill of winter. This was a time for rest and anticipation of the child who would be born in the coming months.

While Matt and the others called this winter, Sean assured him this was mild compared to the winters he survived in the highlands.

"The snow back home will have started falling and will accumulate until spring. There are times when we are snowed in for days," Sean said one night as they sat in front of the blazing fire in the library.

"I swear, Sean, every time you tell that story the snow lasts longer and gets deeper. I remember those winters, but now in the same way as you do," Caleb teased.

"I can relate to Uncle Sean's stories," Matt said. "During the war, there were days when I thought we were going to freeze to death."

"I was only a child," Becky began, "but I remember winters in Philadelphia. There were days when Father couldn't get to the store, so it remained closed until the snow was cleared for people to traverse the streets. I do not miss those days. The weather here is much milder, making winter easier to tolerate."

Matt contemplated the harsh winters he'd endured during the war. He agreed with Becky, he was much happier on the farm than he ever would have been in the north.

Even though Becky engaged in the conversation, he could tell she was tiring. Faking a yawn, he announced it was time for them to go home.

"I don't know why I'm so tired tonight," he said.

"I think you are not completely truthful," Becky teased. "I have never known you to be so tired so early in the evening. I appreciate your concern, but I agree, it's time for us to go home. The further along

I get in this pregnancy, the more active our child becomes. I talked with Summer's Breeze yesterday and she said it normal at this stage of things."

"You all heard my wife. It's time for both of us to retire for the evening. We will see you in the morning. I plan to work with the new mares tomorrow. I'm certain they all carry foals, and I want to check to make certain my assumptions are correct."

Everyone bade them goodnight before they made their way to the home they'd built for themselves.

"It was a delightful evening, the I must admit, I'm glad to be home and have you all to myself for the remainder of the night," Matt commented, once he stoked the fire in the hearth.

"I like being alone with you as well. We must cherish these moments, because when the baby is born, times like these will come at a premium."

"I have a feeling if we desire alone time, my mother as well as Aunt Judith would be more than willing to watch the wee one. It is the one good thing about living so close to my parents."

"You are incorrigible. Once I deliver, James says we must abstain from marriable relations for six weeks. Are you certain you're up for something like that?"

"I, too, have spoken to James about this. He told me it is best if we do not conceive too soon after you give birth. He is thinking of your health as well as the health of our children. In case you haven't noticed, except for Ella's twins, the grandchildren are at least two years apart. When I talked to Soaring Eagle about it, he seemed to agree, as their second child was harder on Summer's Breeze than the first one. We will survive the time when our love making will be little more than hugs and kisses and take precautions to prevent another pregnancy too soon."

"Yesterday, when Summer's Breeze was here, she taught me how to brew a tea to prevent pregnancy until we are ready for a second baby."

Matt held her close, anticipating the upcoming night when they would be enjoying delightful lovemaking. As he did, he felt the child within her womb kick against his hand as though letting him know that within the next few days they would be sharing the woman he loved with all her heart.

~ * ~

Although the wind was cold, Becky insisted they attend church. She knew Matt would have been content staying at home, but he always gave into her wishes.

Along with his parents and aunt and uncle, he and Becky enjoyed the warmth of the blankets they kept in the coach for times like this when taking the carriage was out of the question.

Becky was happy to be out of the house and meeting with friends at church. The first people she saw were her Uncle Richard and Isabelle.

"Are you certain it was wise to come into town when it's so close to your time?" Isabelle asked.

"I tried to tell her the same thing," Matt replied. "After all these years, I've come to realize it's not wise to disagree with her. Coming to church today was very important to her, even though I wouldn't have objected to staying home."

"You are a wise man," Richard declared. "I have been on the receiving end of Becky's ire when she doesn't get her own way. She is a strong woman who has done things her own way for far too many years."

Becky smiled at the backhanded compliment. He knew her too well but had no idea of why she insisted on coming to church this morning. In a dream last night, she envisioned giving birth soon and she needed to confer with James about her premonition.

The last note of the final hymn sounded when the first pains of labor cut through Becky's belly.

"We need to go back to the farm, now. You should also ask James to come out with us."

"Is it the baby? Do you think it is wise to go back to the farm when James' house is so much closer?"

"I have only felt the first pains. I want our child to be born in our home, not in a strange house. With this cold snap I don't want to take him or her out in the weather, when our home is warm and cozy. From everything I have been told by the other women, the first child is never in a hurry to be born. We have plenty of time."

When Caleb and Maude heard of the impending birth, they insisted on returning to the farm with Matt and Becky.

"We do not mean to interfere with your private moment, but Matt looks as nervous as a cat," Caleb told them as he took the driver's seat of the coach. "Besides, I doubt as he is in no condition to drive and still comfort Becky."

Becky agreed with her father-in-law. She was more comfortable with Maude to see to their needs and Caleb driving the coach at what seemed like breakneck speed.

To Becky's surprise, two horses were tied to the railing of the porch, indicating the presence of Soaring Eagle and Summer's Breeze. The two Indians stood on the porch awaiting their arrival.

"Why are you here?" Matt asked, after he helped Becky down from the coach.

"I had a vision last night, brother. In it I saw the birth of your child. Summer's Breeze wanted to be here to be of any help either of you might need. As you know, her mother is a midwife and is teaching Summer's Breeze the same skills."

"Why is it that everyone but me had a premonition that the child would be born today? Why weren't my shaman's powers working like yours are. Even Becky had a dream about the birth of our child."

"You are preoccupied with thoughts of the safety of your wife. It is no wonder you had no visions. We are here now, not only for Brave Woman, but for you as well."

"My brother, James, is on his way, but we appreciate you being here."

With Matt engaged in conversation with his brother, Becky accepted the help of Maude and Summer's Breeze to get into the house and to the upstairs bedroom.

While Maude helped her to undress and put on a fresh gown for the birthing, Summer's Breeze spread a deer skin on the bed to keep for the bedding becoming soiled during the birth.

"What would I do without the two of you?" she asked, between the pains that were becoming stronger with each passing minute.

"You would do what women have done for generations. Childbirth is a natural occurrence, but I am glad that James is on his way here. Should there be any complications, it is best to have a trained doctor in attendance."

From the commotion coming from the first floor, Becky knew more than James had come out to the farm. She listened to the familiar adult voices but didn't hear any of the children.

"We got here as soon as we could," James greeted her. "I want to check and see how the birthing process is progressing. Ma, why don't you go downstairs with the others. Summer's Breeze, I appreciate you being here. I welcome your assistance. I've been told you and your mother are skilled midwives."

Becky stopped listening to their conversation as, yet another stronger pain ripped through her body. Someone screamed and she realized it was her voice, protesting the sensation like no other she'd felt in her life.

"It's time for you to push," James instructed. "This baby is anxious to be outside the confines of your womb and in your loving arms."

With the next three contractions, Becky pushed with all her might. On the third try, her screaming child made its way into the world.

"It's a girl," James declared, as Summer's Breeze cleansed the baby in the warm water Maude brought up moments ago.

~ * ~

No amount of comforting could calm Matt's nerves. He didn't like the idea of Becky being in such pain even though he knew it was part of bringing forth life.

"Would it help if we prayed?" Thomas suggested.

Matt shook his head no and continued to pace the length of the sitting room.

"Pacing will not bring the child into the world any sooner," Soaring Eagle said. "You do nothing more than wear out the carpet Becky insisted on having in this room. Both times Summer's Breeze gave birth, I celebrated with the other men of the village. I certainly didn't walk back and forth in front of our lodge."

Everyone laughed at soaring Eagle's description of how differently things were done in the Indian village. Their laughter ceased when Becky's scream of pain tore through the entire house.

"This is all my fault," Matt lamented.

"Nothing is your fault," Maude consoled him. "It is natural and believe me, once Becky holds the baby, the memory of the pain will fade from her mind. It will become nothing more than a pleasant memory of that which is natural for your child to be born."

After what seemed like a lifetime to Matt, Becky's screams of pain were replaced with a different cry. This one told him their child had finally entered the world and was protesting the cooler temperature outside of its mother's body.

Several minutes later, James came downstairs. "You have a beautiful daughter. She has a tuft of dark hair and the bluest eyes I have ever seen. Becky came through her ordeal like a trouper. Summer's Breeze is cleaning up the baby and Becky. They insisted I should get out of the way and come down to advise you of her birth."

Matt was so overwhelmed with the safety of Becky and their yet to be named daughter, he dropped to his knees in exhaustion and prayer. "Can I go up and see them?" he finally managed to ask.

"Summer's Breeze will come for you when they are ready for company. She was of great help with the birth. I wish she could accompany me whenever I need to attend a birthing mother."

Matt watched as his brothers, James and Soaring Eagle, shook hands in true friendship. In Soaring Eagle's eyes, he could see pride at the compliment given to his wife for the help she was able to give.

Moments turned into minutes and lingered into almost half an hour before Summer's Breeze came downstairs. Seeing her, Matt didn't hesitate to take the stairs two at a time to get to the side of his wife and daughter.

He tapped lightly on the door; aware the baby might be sleeping.

"Get in here and meet your daughter," Becky called from behind the closed door.

In their big bed, Becky beamed in the afterglow of giving birth. In her arms, the tiny baby lay swaddled in the brilliant yellow blanket his mother made from the softest material the store had to offer. Although her complexion was ruddy, he knew that could change as the ordeal of coming into the world passed and a more natural color appeared. A shock of dark hair graced her head and as James told him, the most beautiful blue eyes he'd ever seen looked at him as though she recognized him as her father.

"James was right, she is a perfect baby."

"Let's see if you say the same thing when she awakens in the middle of the night demanding to be fed. If she's anything like her father, she will have a ferocious appetite."

"Do you know what we will name her?"

"I am hoping you will approve of us calling her Winter Lee. Winter to honor your people and to designate the time of the year when she has come into the world and Lee to carry on a tradition in my family. My mother's middle name was Lee, as is mine. It is only fitting she carry it as well."

"I think it fits her properly."

As though Winter knew they were talking about her, she wigged one little hand free to grab onto Matt's finger.

"We make quite the family," Becky said. "Hawk, Brave Woman and Winter will form our own tribe. Between the three of us, we share the best genes of our races and Winter is a mixture of the two of us. No one would ever dare to call her a savage. It was only fitting that your brother and Summer's Breeze were here to help her find her way into the world."

Matt could tell Becky was tiring and even Winter yawned, exhausted by the ordeal of birth. Once they were both peacefully sleeping, he left the room and went down to join his family in celebration.

"We have a granddaughter," Maude said when he entered the room. "Are you disappointed she is not a boy."

"There is nothing about Winter that is a disappointment. She is destined for great things as a bridge between the people who have occupied this land for generations and those who have come to settle and begin new lives. We are calling her Winter Lee to honor both sides of her heritage."

"You have made a wise choice in names, Hawk," Soaring Eagle said. "With a name that honors our people, she will always be welcome and cherished in our village. Now that we know all is well, Summer's Breeze and I will return to our lodge. Our children will be anxious to be in their own beds, and it is best we return to the village before the darkness becomes the black of night. As you know, it is dangerous to travel long distances at night."

Everyone agreed with Soaring Eagle's logic. As for the MacAfee family, they would be celebrating throughout the night. With the children secure in town with members of the church congregation, everyone would be spending the night at the main house.

Although many toasts were made, Matt refrained from drinking the brandy his father, Sean and James were enjoying. Instead, he nursed a glass of wine for a while before retiring to the bedroom where he left Becky and Winter to their well-deserved nap.

The last rays of afternoon sunlight lit the room in a soft glow. Even so he could tell Becky and Winter were awake. The baby nursed taking the necessary nourishment from her mother's body.

After lighting the lamp on the bedside table, Matt sat down on his side of the bed. "I've never seen a more enduring sight in my life."

"You'll get used to it. Summer's Breeze says I will be nursing Winter for the next year. I must admit, Winter instinctively knew exactly what to do. She is also quite vocal when she wants to be fed."

"I know it's impossible, but I wish I was able to feed her. I want to form a bond with her as soon as possible."

"When you are not busy, we will make a good team. I will feed her, and you will burp her. Don't worry, I'll teach you what to do. You will have your own special time as father and daughter, even though you cannot give her nourishment. Instead, you will relieve the air bubbles she swallows when she eats."

~ * ~

Long after Becky and Winter slept peacefully, Matt lay awake. The only thing he knew about giving birth was helping the mares to deliver their colts. In the world of horses, the stud would have no part in raising its offspring. In the pasture they would be kept away from the colts to keep from either fighting with the males for supremacy or trying to mount the females. They would never know which of the colts they fathered, nor would they for any sort of bond with them.

For tonight, Winter belonged to only Becky and him. In the morning Winter would to be introduced to the rest of her extended family. By noon everyone in town would know of the long-awaited baby had arrived.

Finally, he joined Becky and Winter in sleep. He didn't think he was tired enough to sleep soundly, but soon he was asleep and with it came prophetic dreams. In those dreams, he saw he and Becky surrounded by children. Like his parents before them, not all the children were ones they gave birth to, but orphans who needed the love of two parents.

Chapter Twenty-Two
Five years later

The end of summer loomed. Matt and Becky sat on the porch of their home, enjoying the quiet of the Sunday afternoon.

Their son, Marcus Full Moon, toddled after Winter on unsteady legs. She had taken on the role of a little mother and guided her baby brother in everything he did.

"I heard Jenny Adams recently gave birth only to die in the process. Her husband wants nothing to do with the child and plans to move out of the area soon," Becky said. "Do you think…?"

Matt put his finger to her lips. "You aren't finished nursing Marcus. Are you sure you want to take on the responsibility of another baby?"

"Positive. We have the room for another child and enough love to share. What if your parents hadn't taken you in? What would have become of you, to say nothing of Ella and Susan? We all know the farmers in this area are more interested in having boys to carry their family name and work on the farm. They do not hold girls in such high esteem."

"With Jenny dying in childbirth, who is caring for the child?"

"Mrs. Campbell, but with the size of her brood, she doesn't want to take on another baby."

"You are still nursing Marcus. Do you think you will have enough for two children?"

"Marcus is almost weaned. Have you not noticed he often wants milk in a cup to be like Winter. He walked much earlier than she did. He wants to grow up too fast."

"Do you have a name in mind?"

"Not until I see and hold her. It is then that I will know what to name her. I am hoping the name Swallow Ann will fit her, but only time will tell."

"I never told you, but on the night of Winter's birth, I saw us surrounded by many children and not all of them ours by blood, but by love. I didn't know how you would react to my vision."

"I have learned to trust your visions. I have even been granted one of two of them. Do you think your parents would watch the children while we go into town to fetch our new daughter. Knowing you agree with me, I can't stand the thoughts of her not being with us as soon as possible."

Matt enjoyed the look of excitement on Becky's face. He knew no matter what she asked, he could never tell her no. The thought of having another daughter to love excited him as well.

~ * ~

As soon as Becky held the small baby in her arms, she knew the name she chose without seeing the child was perfect for her. Swallow Ann matched the child's petite features. Rather than dark hair, her head was covered with downy blonde fuzz. She would be in direct contrast to her older sister.

"We must take her over to the church and see if Thomas will baptize her. I want her to carry our name as soon as possible."

They found Thomas in the rectory, preparing the sermon for Sunday's upcoming service, "I was hoping James would convince you to increase your family in this unusual way. Had you not been receptive to the idea, I am afraid she would have been placed with a family who would not easily accept her as one of their own."

"We are hoping you would baptize her before we take her back to the farm," Becky said.

"Of course I will. It will strengthen the bond between the child and her new family. I would expect nothing less of you, considering the children your father took as his own so many years ago. What name have you chosen?'

"Swallow Ann. The swallow is a delicate little bird and as you can see, she's a tiny little thing."

"You may be surprised if she grows enough to no longer be considered petite. James told me she was born earlier than is natural due to a complication with the pregnancy. Even with his expertise, he couldn't save the mother. Her husband is planning the funeral for tomorrow, then he is leaving the area. He has already signed papers saying he wants nothing to do with the baby. I'm certain he will be pleased to know she is being placed with a loving family."

Becky's heart ached for the tiny baby who lost her mother so tragically and had a father who wanted nothing to do with her. "Never fear, little Swallow, you will know nothing but love for the rest of your life. From this day forward Hawk and I will be your parents. Winter and Marcus will be delighted with their new sister."

~ * ~

On the trip back to the farm, Becky nursed the baby. When she finished eating, Matt reached for his new daughter. As was his habit, he burped the baby, sealing his bond with the child.

"While Thomas was baptizing our new daughter, I was giving God a prayer of thanksgiving for bringing this child into our lives."

"We are blessed with this child. I fell in love with her the first time I held her. I can't believe it wasn't the same way with Mrs. Campbell. Of course, she has her hand full with seven children of her own. As far as I can see Mr. Campbell is more interested in making children than caring for them."

As soon as they pulled into the door yard, they were greeted by Caleb and Maude with the children in tow.

"Grandpa said you went to town to get us a new baby sister. Can we keep her?" Winter asked.

"Forever and always," Matt assured her.

"What's her name?"

"Swallow Ann," Becky replied.

"Swallow Ann," Winter repeated. "I like it. I came in the winter, and the swallow is a summer bird. She's tiny, just like the swallows in the stable. I can hardly wait until she's old enough to play with Marcus and me."

"That will take a while," Matt told her. "In the meantime, you can help your mother."

The answer seemed to pacify the little girl.

"I see you are following in our footsteps," Caleb said as Maude cooed over the baby. "Children are always welcome on this farm, regardless of their parentage. I understand why Hunting Hawk couldn't take you with him on that first night, but he remained in your life. What I don't understand how a man can sign a paper giving away his child. I wonder if he would have felt the same way if she had been born a boy."

"I doubt it," Becky replied. "I knew Jenny well and often she would have unexplained bruises. I was but I child and didn't understand anything but I do remember my mother having bruises she tried to explain away after my parents would have a fight. I'm afraid Jenny's husband was beating her and that was why she gave birth early. It could be part of the reason she died giving birth."

"I don't understand men who would do something like that," Caleb declared. "I was taught women are precious and should be treated with the greatest of care."

Becky shook her head in dismay. "Unfortunately, I know firsthand about men who beat their wives. At the time I didn't understand what was happening, but I now realize my father beat my mother with great regularity. I don't know how I escaped his wrath, but he never touched me in such a manner."

She surprised herself by admitting things her father was guilty of doing. Never had she told anyone of the abuse her mother suffered. Just the thought of what transpired in Philadelphia made her sick to her stomach.

"Enough of this sad talk," she said. "It is time for Swallow to eat and settle into the cradle."

The children followed her into the house and watched as she bared her breast to nurse the baby. Marcus looked at his mother longingly and seemed to understand he was no longer a baby needing to take nourishment from his mother's body. He left the setting room and ran into the kitchen, returning with the cup she'd been urging him to use at meals.

"Big boy cup," he declared.

"Yes, my darling boy, you are a big boy now. This type of feeding is how Swallow will take her nourishment now."

"Baby sister," he said, rubbing her head of blonde fuzz before running off to play.

"I expected him to be jealous of Swallow taking to your breast," Matt said.

"I thought there might be some tears, but I have been introducing the cup for his milk at meals. He wants to be so much like Winter; it didn't take him long to understand that big boys didn't nurse from their mothers. He's growing up so fast and is proud of each new accomplishment. It won't be long before you must find a pony for him, like you did for Winter. I'm certain he is anxious to learn how ride if for no other reason than to do something his sister so enjoys."

~ * ~

Soaring Eagle returned from the trading post with the supplies Summer's Breeze asked him to procure for her. As he neared the village, he contemplated the information he'd been given by the storekeeper.

It didn't seem possible for Hawk and Brave Woman to have another child. As far as he knew they were not expecting another baby. It didn't make sense until he learned the little girl they called Swallow was an orphan. Her mother had died giving birth, not unlike Hawk's true mother, and her father disowned the child.

In the past he'd heard stories of Phineas Adams and none of them were good. It was well known that some of the young braves had been out hunting when they heard cries from the Adams cabin. Upon further inspection, they witnessed Phineas beating his wife.

Wisely, they gave the cabin a wide birth and returned to the village. They'd learned not to interfere in things the white men in the area participated in. It was entirely possible such a beating would have brought on the early birth of the child and the death of her mother during childbirth.

It was no wonder Hawk and Brave Woman made no hesitation in taking Swallow to raise as their own. He was paying back the kindness shown to him by Caleb so many years earlier.

"We must go to visit Hawk and Brave Woman, he announced to Summer's Breeze, as they shared the evening meal.

"Has something happened to them?" she asked.

"You might say that."

He went on to explain the story of how they had taken an orphaned child into their home to raise as their own.

"She is a very lucky little girl. There is no one else I know who would take in an orphaned child. Do you know what they named her?"

"Swallow Ann. The storekeeper told me they took her to the white man's church and had her baptized before they left the village."

"Speaking of the white man's church, have you given any more thought to what the missionary said when he met with the elders several days ago?"

Soaring Eagle turned his thoughts from his brother's family to the meeting that had many in the village in turmoil.

"I know he wants us to give up the old ways, but the shaman says he has had a vision, saying the white man's God and the Great Spirit are one in the same. In the stories the ancestors have passed down to us tell much the same thing as what the missionary is preaching. I have been conferring with the shaman, and we have concluded if we are to live close to the white village, we should conform to their God. Like the Great Spirit, he preaches about love for your fellow man and doing no evil to your neighbors. If he wants us to be baptized, I would not object."

"I was hoping that would be your answer. Many of the women have been considering the same thing. I didn't know how to suggest it to you. I want to have the children baptized as well. Especially since Brave Woman told me of how they celebrated when Winter and Marcus were baptized. I do enjoy planning a feast and I cannot think of a better reason for one, than this."

~ * ~

Matt was surprised when his brother, with his family, rode into the door yard. Just a few hours earlier, he told Becky that they needed to send a message to Soaring Eagle to announce the arrival of Swallow. She'd already been in their home for a week and immediately became a cherished member. Having a new baby in the house meant more work for Becky as well as himself. It was only this morning when he thought of sending a message to his brother.

"Is everything well in the village?"

"I asked the same thing of you when I was at the trading post. I was surprised when I heard of a new baby in your household. I must say, I was confused about Swallow's arrival, since I didn't think you and Brave Woman were expecting. That was when the storekeeper told me the story of her being orphaned. Who other than you would understand the necessity of someone giving her a loving home?"

Matt laughed at his brother's statement. "We were talking this morning at breakfast when I realized I hadn't advised you of Swallow's arrival. She is a real joy in our lives. It was something that needed to be done, since Becky was still nursing Marcus."

"I worried about that," Summer's Breeze said. "How did he take giving up nursing for another baby? Usually, a woman doesn't nurse two children at a time."

"We worried about that too, but the day we brought Swallow home, he went to the kitchen and got the cup Becky has been urging him to use and declared he was a big boy."

"Don't keep our company waiting outside. I can smell rain in the air. Bring them into the house. I have fresh coffee bread made and a pot of coffee on the stove. I also have cookies for the children. I know how much they love my sugar cookies."

"You do have a tendency to spoil the children, Brave Woman," Soaring Eagle declared. "Did you anticipate our arrival?"

"I should have, but I know my children love sugar cookies the same as yours do. I bake for them almost every day. The coffee bread is one that Matt enjoys. He has as much of a sweet tooth as the children."

Matt called for one of the stable boys to see to the horses as he watched his brother and his family go into the house. It took a while before Soaring Eagle and Summer's Breeze to take advantage of the hospitality Becky extended. As for the children, they were always anxious to play with Winter and Marcus.

"I swear these children are growing like weeds," Summer's Breeze declared. "You must feed them well."

Marcus grabbed two cookies from the plate saying 'cookie' as he and Winter took their cousins to the playroom.

Summer's Breeze was pleased to see how well the children got along when they were together. Theirs would always be a bond the closed the gap between the people and those of the white world.

"I'm so glad you brought the children," Becky said, as she cut thick slices of coffee bead. "Winter and Markus enjoy having them visit."

Summer's Breeze nodded as she tasted the sweet bread that was laced with cinnamon, sugar and raisins. It was so unlike any bread she made for her family. Like the children, she did enjoy the sweet treats Becky always seemed to have on hand.

"Swallow should be waking from her morning nap soon. Would you like to meet her?"

"You know I would. She is a lucky little girl to have you and Hawk to give your love to her."

~ * ~

Matt and Soaring Eagle took their coffee and thick slices of coffee bread with them out to the stable.

"As usual you have some of the finest horses in the area. The mares and stallion your father brought from Scotland are magnificent. I hope you are getting well compensated for their offspring."

"Never worry about that. Pa is quite the negotiator when it comes to the sale of horses. I have been learning from him how to obtain the best price. Is your herd increasing?"

"They are, but none of them are for sale. The more horses I have the richer I am among the people. I now meet with Running Deer daily. He values my opinion as much as I value him.

"I noticed how Marcus is growing. Have you picked out a pony for him to ride? I doubt it won't be long before he wants to be like his sister."

"Becky and I were talking about that the other day. One of the mares gave birth to a fine little filly. By the time Marcus is ready to learn how to ride, she will be perfect for him."

Epilogue
Ten years later

Matt and Becky lingered over their morning coffee. He marveled at how his life changed in such a short time.

Two years after Swallow joined their family, his mother passed away in her sleep. James said it was a massive heart attack, and she felt no pain in her passing.

Even so, Matt watched as his father's health declined. Litte by little, the light began to go out in Caleb's eyes. He no longer went down to the stable and insisted Matt; Becky and the children move to the main house to keep him company. Before even a year passed, he followed Maude to the grave. Jame's conclusion was the same ailment as took their mother, but Matt suspected it was a broken heart.

There had never been anything but love between his parents. In other words, Caleb wanted no part of life without Maude in it.

Matt turned his thoughts to his family. He loved Becky with all his heart. Next came his children. Winter was growing into the exotic beauty he'd predicted at her birth. Her dark hair was in direct contrast to the sky blue of her eyes. Many young men showed an interest in courting her, but her answer was always the same, she wasn't ready for any sort of relationship. Her love, like that of her father and grandfather, was MacAfee farm and the prime horses they produced.

Marcus was in the process of becoming a young man. Like his sister, he loved everything about MacAfee farm but was more interested in accounting and dealing with the buyers. As an adult, he would be a shrewd businessman following in the same footsteps of his mother.

The last of his children, Swallow, was far different from her siblings. She was becoming a beauty in her own right. Her goal in life was to be a wife and mother. In preparation, she spent hours learning to cook and sew. She would, one day, have a family and make them proud of the woman she became.

"A penny for your thoughts," Becky said, interrupting his inner musings.

"I was thinking of the past and envisioning the future. I see myself in Winter. Her love of working with horses and running this farm comes from me. She is also close to my brother, Soaring Eagle and his family.

"Marcus is your son. He has your mind for business and little thought of the daily duties of managing the farm. One day he will make more progress in selling our horses than either my father or I ever did.

"That leaves only Swallow. Although we raised her from almost the day of her birth, she is more like Jenny. She wants nothing more than a home and family of her own. She will be an excellent wife and mother."

"Those are deep thoughts for so early in the morning. I agree with everything you've said. When the time is right, we will have to let each of them follow their own paths in this life. I hope we can keep them close to us, if not on the farm, in the village. I foresee many grandchildren in our lives."

Matt pulled Becky into a warm embrace. They were two people sharing one heart's desire. They would be together, forever, surrounded by the family they both loved.

www.ingramcontent.com/pod-product-compliance
Lightning Source LLC
Chambersburg PA
CBHW040905010826
48978CB00013BB/1154